Rock of Ages
A Journey through Life

A Novel

Richard D. Reavis

Acknowledgements

After doing a final reading I thought back at the hours spent crafting this story. I can't help but dwell on those who have had an integral part in the process. First of all, we give all the credit to God through whom all things are possible. He is our true source of inspiration. I thank my wife, Bonnie, who has stood beside me over the last six decades. Her unwavering support as a sounding board gave me encouragement to push through to the end. To my granddaughter, Aurora, who edited the book in lightning speed: what a great job you did. To the rest of my children and grandchildren who encouraged their dad and grandpa to reach outside his comfort zone, I am forever grateful. Finally, I want to thank my son, Donald, for his willingness to publish Rock of Ages. It has been an exciting adventure. Now, as I sit here holding a prepress copy of Rock of Ages, I am humbled and blessed by the hours so many others have selflessly given to make it possible. Thank you.

The Author

Table of Contents

Prologue

It was a beautiful fall day and Amos was doing the chores at the barn. The hired men were husking corn in the field, and Alice had just finished bringing in the last of the garden. As she went up the steps onto the porch, she noticed Amos running towards the road. She was perplexed, as he hardly ever ran anymore. It seemed he was running towards what looked like someone coming down the road. Who could it be to make him run like that?

The Happy Home
Chapter One

Life on the farm was a busy one. There was always plenty to do. Amos Wagoner and his wife, Alice, had two sons: John, who was ten years old and Sam, who was eight. Besides the large acreage of cotton, and the fields of corn, they also had a lot of cattle and many sheep. The workload justified hiring a few men to help out around the farm.

John was a quiet type of a boy, somewhat reserved, and would always obey. Sam was very outgoing, boisterous, and not inclined to always obey. As they grew up, John liked to read whenever he could, but always did his chores cheerfully, and promptly. Sam would have to be asked at least twice to do his chores. Sam was an outdoors type of a boy, and was good at sports. John found it hard to compete with his little brother. Sometimes when they would play ball and Sam would win, it would make John angry, and he didn't always treat his brother as he should.

Amos and Alice were followers of the Lord, and thankful for the blessings that were afforded to them. They arose early in the morning, Amos went to the barn to do the chores, while Alice started breakfast, and called the boys to get up. John always arose on the first call, while many times Sam had to be called a second time. The boys had chores to do and didn't always like doing them. It was even tougher when they had been out late the night before, and it was later than usual before they got to bed. Or when it was cold and under the covers felt so good. However, they always made their way down the stairs and out to the barn.

John milked the cow, and fed the young calves. He enjoyed teaching a newborn calf to drink from a bucket. He looked forward to the days when he went to the barn, and there was a new calf standing by its mother. He would give it a name, and then ask dad if that would be okay. Most of the times it was okay, but occasionally there was another cow with that name, so between him and dad they would think of another name. These calves were special to him.

Sam had the responsibility of tending to the sheep. He would take the bucket of grain into the lot, and call them, and they would come running. Bleating as they came, the sheep knew he had their breakfast. Some of them would rub against him, like he was their best friend. He would make sure they had plenty of clean water. It was a highlight when he came out and saw there was a new little lamb. He would laugh as he watched their wobbly long legs. He called them "my sheep". When the early chores were done, they returned to the house. As they opened the door, aah, the aroma of the breakfast their dear mother had waiting for them. After washing up and having seated themselves at the table, they bowed their heads, while Amos thanked the Lord for all the blessings he gave them.

As they enjoyed the food, they discussed the day's work ahead: what needed to be done, who would do what and how to do it. After they were done eating, Amos picked up the Bible, read a chapter, and then explained it. If anyone had a question he would give an answer to it. Often John, being a serious minded young man, would have one, which made Sam a little agitated. He wanted to go outside, and get going.

Sometimes there were surprises for them, as the day when dad said his brother and family were coming to their place this afternoon, and staying for a couple of days. Sam said, "Hurray" and was very excited. To think his cousin, Enos, who was just six days younger then he, was coming for two days. John was not as excited, as there wasn't a boy his age. The oldest of Uncle Ronald and Aunt Sarah's children was a girl named Joyce, a year older than he, and a boy named Thomas, one year younger.

He knew they would have an enjoyable time, as they always did when Uncle Ronald's came. Dad said, "Boys, get your work done up as much as you can, and help mom well. Mother and I talked it over, and if it is alright with Uncle Ronald's, we plan to have an outing back in the woods by the pond. We'll take dinner and have a wiener roast. We can take the fishing poles and go fishing. We can walk through the woods, pick some flowers, and watch for wild life too." The boys were so happy, and Amos overheard them say, "Aren't we a happy family!"

Uncle Ronald's came as planned, arriving about four in the afternoon. After a bit of hand shaking, hugs and kisses, they took their suit cases and all went into the house.

John and Sam wanted to show their cousins the animals, so the children went to the barn. John took the older children to see the calves, while Sam and Enos looked in on the sheep. They were all delighted with the animals. There were twin lambs just a day old, which hopped around. Enos thought they were so cute with their long thin wobbly legs. Sam invited his cousin to help feed the little lambs. Joyce and Thomas were impressed with the calves John was taking care of. He let them pet some of them.

"Tomorrow I'll show you how to teach them how to drink out of a bucket." John told them. The children heard the call for supper time and headed for the house.

They gathered at the dining room table, and Amos said, "We feel so blessed to have you folks at our table, and the Lord has been with us the years we have been apart. Let's sing a verse of, *Nearer My God to Thee.*" His deep voice started the song, and they all joined in. Then Amos asks Uncle Ronald to thank the Lord for their blessings, and to ask a blessing on the food. Uncle Ronald, being a minister, prayed a beautiful prayer.

After supper, the children told mom and Aunt Sarah to go in the living room and catch up on their news, while they would do the dishes. As they washed and dried the dishes they sang some beautiful songs of praise. After the work was finished they played some games, and too soon it was time to go to bed.

The next morning, after the chores were done, they all gathered around the dining room table to a breakfast of ham and eggs, with coffee and orange juice. Uncle Ronald again had a nice morning prayer. Then Amos approached them concerning their plans of a cookout at the pond. Uncle Ronald and Aunt Sarah said that sounded like a nice thing to do. After all were done eating, Ronald read Psalm ninety.

While the ladies cleaned up the breakfast things, and got the food ready to go for the picnic, the men finished up the chores. They took the sides off the flat bed wagon and harnessed the horses, hitching them to the wagon. The boys got the fishing poles and dug up a few worms. The boxes of food, and chairs for the older folks, were stacked in the center of the wagon and they all sat around the outside with their legs dangling over the edge. Amos and Ronald, seated at the front, drove the team down the lane to the woods by the pond.

The two days passed quickly, and they all had an enjoyable time. Thomas loved helping John feed the calves. John taught him how to break a calf to bucket drink. Joyce, being a bookworm, told John of some good books to read, even brought some along and left them with him.

Working on the farm was hard and tiring but rewarding. Alice had a large garden, which took a lot of work. As a girl, she remembered having to hoe for hours, all by herself. Not wanting the boys to go through the same lonely experience, she would take one at a time when she went to hoe. She would show him how to use a hoe correctly, and how to do a good job. Then she would work beside him, and they would talk as they worked. That made it not seem as hard of a job.

One morning after breakfast, Amos said he was going over to husk corn for a neighbor who had broken his leg. He asked Alice if she could spare Sam, as he wanted him to go along. John had previously committed to helping another neighbor that day. Alice said she thought it would be good for him. After hitching the horses to the box wagon they headed up the road. Amos handed the reins to Sam, "You drive." Sam was delighted, as this was his first time to drive horses. Amos showed him how to turn corners, and how to keep them on the road. Sam thought, "Life with dad is grand." They had a very enjoyable day working together. Sam learned how to husk corn using a husking knife. He couldn't keep up with his dad, but he tried and worked hard. They got two loads of corn husked and into the crib.

Sam asked his dad about the mask on the horse closest to the first standing row of corn. Amos explained how a horse in a corn field, is like boys at a candy dish; they will eat too much and get sick. The horse next to the row has ears of corn beside him all the time. The temptation to grab an ear is too great and too much corn will make him sick. The muzzle keeps him from doing that. Amos let Sam drive all the way home, and he made no mistakes. He sure was a happy boy.

Winter soon set in. It snowed all day, and by chore time eight inches of wet snow covered the ground. They were on their way to the house when a neighbor and his son came over to talk to Amos. While they talked, the three boys made a circle in the snow and started to play fox and geese. They asked their dads to play with them, which they did. It was so much fun, and even more so to be playing with their fathers. To watch them fall down, laugh, get up and go on, was about as much fun for the boys as it was to play, however the most enjoyment came from playing with their dads. They felt it was a privilege and were very happy.

The years passed by, and each year they grew older and were changed more and more. One day, the first of December, Mom asked John if he would like to make some candy for Christmas. He wasn't too sure, as cooking wasn't what he was used to doing. He did like candy, so he said he would. He and his mother made some peanut brittle and fudge. At fourteen years old he was used to working hard in the field, and spending a lot of time with his father, but it was a privilege to work with his mother. He learned some things. He had a happy day!

The next week Mom asked Sam if he would like to make candy too. He jumped at the chance. He made more of a mess than John, but Alice didn't say anything about it. Both of them were enjoying working together. They made three kinds of candy and some popcorn balls. He thought, "What fun, what a happy day!"

The Ball Game
Chapter 2

John enjoyed the books his cousin left him, but it seemed he didn't have much time to read. Most days by the time he got his chores done and breakfast was over, then devotions, it was time for school. He liked school, and he made good grades. Sometimes after he got done with his school for the day, he needed to go and clean out calf pens and bed them. That took a lot of time, but if he wanted to have healthy calves he knew he must keep them clean and dry.

Sam didn't like school, even though he wanted to learn, it went hard for him. It took longer for him finish his lessons. As a result he had less time in the afternoon to care for his sheep. By the time they got the work all done, it was supper time. After supper they would go to the barn and close the doors to the pens. By the time they returned to the house it would be time for devotions. Some evenings mother wanted the family to sing, which both boys enjoyed. The whole family were good singers. A singing family is usually a happy family.

Many times while they were working out in the barn Alice would hear the boys singing with all their hearts. The sheep and the calves were used to that.

One day Sam was having trouble getting the gate to close right. He said, "There needs to be two of me!"

Just then John came around the barn and said, "If you would just ask, I would help you." The two of them soon got it fixed.

Sam said, "Thank you, and by the way, you said if I had asked, now I will ask, would you play pitch and catch with me after supper?"

John replied, "I was hoping to have time to read more of that good book Joyce left with me, but yes, if we have time, I'll do that."

Sam said, "Let's work hard and help each other and maybe we'll get done early and can play a little catch before supper." By working hard and helping each other, they had an hour to play before supper. Sam could throw well and was a good catcher, but it went hard for John.

Sam told their dad when they came in for supper that John needed to practice more. Amos said, "Maybe we can arrange for you boys to practice for an hour or so in the afternoon." That suited Sam, John would have liked to read more, but he did play some in the time their father gave them.

One day the neighbor boys came over and wanted to get a ball game going. The boys had been working hard, so Amos told them they could have the afternoon off. The hired men could take care of their chores. The neighbors had eight boys old enough to play ball, so there were enough for two teams. When they chose up teams, John and Sam ended up on the same team, but John was the last to be chosen. This didn't make him feel too good, but he knew it was because they all knew he couldn't catch a ball, or hit very well.

Their team was the first to go to bat. The bases were loaded with two outs when it was John's turn to bat. The first pitch was a foul ball. The second pitch he didn't swing for he thought it was outside, but the umpire said it was a strike. He swung at the third pitch for all he had and missed. They were out. John held his head down in shame, and Sam showed his anger to his brother. Another time when they were on outfield, and the bases were loaded, a fly ball came right to John, which he should have been able to catch, but he fumbled it, so the opposing team made a home run.

John did make a few runs, and once even made a home run, but it was Sam which showed the best for their team. They lost by three points, and John felt it was his fault. Sam sort of pointed that out too, which made him feel even worse. John tried, and he sometimes did better, but almost always it was Sam that excelled in sports.

The Spelling Bee
Chapter 3

John and Sam were home schooled with their mother as their teacher. Sam, not liking books, had trouble with spelling.

One day the neighbor boys came over along with their four sisters. They wanted to practice their spelling together. Once they had studied a section of the book they asked Alice to test them. They all lined up along the wall. The first word was given, and it was a girl who spelled it correct. The next word was to Sam and it was "believe" and he said, "Believe, b-e-i-l-e-v-e believe". Mother said, "Wrong!" Sam had to sit down. The next was another girl and she spelled it correct. Most of the words were spelled correct, so this made Sam feel humble as he had no one else sitting down with him. When the words became harder, some failed to say "Capital," before spelling a proper name, others got letters inverted, and some just couldn't spell the word.

All had been spelled down, except three of the girls, and one of the neighbor boys, and John. These five were spelling all the words correctly, so Mother gave them the word, "consistent," and down went one girl and the other boy. Then John spelled it correctly. Now there were two girls and John. The next word was, "justification" and one of the girls missed it, but the other one got it right. Then there were several words that both could spell, Finally Mother gave them the word "Nebuchadnezzar." The girl tried, and almost got it right, but she left out one z. Then John spelled it right, but Mother said that he heard the girl almost spell it right, so he should spell another hard word, to be the winner, so she gave him the word, "Belteshazzar", and he spelled it correctly.

Sam told him, after the neighbors left, that he didn't have to act so smart in front of all of them. John said, "That is the way you did after the ball game the other day." Brotherly love didn't grow any from these occasional animosities.

One evening after supper as the family were gathered around the family altar, Amos brought up the subject about the ball game, and the spelling bee. He told them, "Not all people are alike, nor have the same talents. What talents we have are given to us by God, however, we have the responsibility to develop them to the best of our ability. Never should we look down on those who don't have the same ability as we have." Then he had a story to tell them about a little red wagon, and the mud hole.

"There were two little boys with a little red wagon. Most of the time, they played together nice. One of the boys was riding in the wagon as the other was pulling him when they went into a mud hole, and the wagon got stuck. They didn't know how to get it out. The boy in the wagon got out and he thought they should push it back the way they came in, but the other one said that they should go on through as that would be closer. They were both sure the way they thought was the right way, so when their father came home he found them, one on the front and the other on the back, both pushing as hard as they could, but to no avail. He said, boys, you must work together or you'll never get out."

Amos told John, and Sam, "Those boys both wanted to play with the wagon, which they agreed on. They wanted it out of the mud, which they agreed on. They didn't agree on how to achieve this goal, nor were they willing to submit to the other one. Because of this disagreement they couldn't play with their wagon. If they would have worked together either way would probably have worked, but to work against each other will always cause difficulty.

Then he read to them the condensed story of Joseph and how he was treated by his brothers. How he forgave them, when he had seen their repentance and sorrow. How he loved them, in spite of how they had hated him. Then they all knelt together and prayed to the Heavenly Father to guide their ways into the truth. They slept well knowing their father was a loving dad and wanted them to walk with the people of God.

The Inheritance
Chapter 4

The years rolled by and the boys were seventeen and nineteen. Being more of adult age, they were needed in the field to help the farm hands. John didn't seem to mind, as he saw they were getting ahead financially. The farm was paid off and they had a lot of cattle and sheep. His dad was well liked by the workers, as he was kind and paid them fair. Some of them had worked on the farm for several years, and they never went hungry, or were in need of anything.

Sunday mornings always found them going to church. Amos was a deacon, and helped to start the songs. This Sunday was a special day, as there were three young people to be baptized. John was one of them, which made his parents rejoice. Sam felt, someday he too would do that.

Both boys were in the young folks now, and they most always attended the singings on Sunday evenings. John would start some of the songs. He had a deep voice like his dad. These songs were deep in meaning, and lifted their minds heavenward, as they praised God. At these young folk's singings, some of the younger boys, being away from their parents, would not come in for a while. At times instead of singing they would whisper and snicker, which was distracting. Even though Sam had always liked to sing, the fun the boys were having, lured him a little at a time, away from the seriousness of the meeting. There were times when some of them didn't come in at all.

One of the boys went to public school, and he had some bad stories to tell them, which made them laugh. One day that boy somehow got some cigarettes and some of the boys smoked them behind the barn. If any of the boys would reprimand them, they would call him "preacher boy", and make sport of him. Sam thought these boys were the life of the young folks. He knew his dad wouldn't approve of that type of thing, but dad wasn't there. Besides, he hadn't taken a cigarette, or told any dirty stories, but he liked the laughs.

Somehow after hearing these dirty stories and jokes for awhile, he couldn't get them out of his mind. Soon he was also telling them. This made him popular to do so. A boy offered him a cigarette one time, and when he refused it he was called, "Goody boy, goody boy, 'suppose you're going to tell on us." Sam broke down and took one.

Over time, at home Sam felt it was just work, and not much play. Why, with all the money his folks had, why couldn't they have more fun? His attitude became a problem for his folks, and they talked to him about it. Sometimes his mother would cry, as he would be contentious. His dad kept pleading with him. He talked to him about Joseph, also the story of the wagon in the mud, but Sam was getting worse. He wanted to see the world.

The day Sam turned eighteen he wanted to talk to his folks. He told them that he was now of age and wanted his inheritance. Amos tried to reason with him, but to no avail. When they had their evening devotions, a lot of times Sam wouldn't be there, and nobody knew where he was.

Of a morning he would sit there when Amos read from the Bible, with an arrogant look on his face, which made his mother sad, but he didn't seem to care. It appeared as if his heart had become bitter. What could they do?

They were thankful that John wasn't like that, nor had he ever been. He seemed to have an interest in the farm and was a good worker, never complaining. Never did he disobey what his parents told him. Why couldn't Sam be like him?

Amos and Alice decided to give the boys their inheritance, so they divided the things up and gave it to them. Sam wanted his in cash, so they sold some of the livestock, and gave him his share. The farm went to John.

In a few days Sam took his entire possessions and left home, not to be seen for a long while. He was so bitter, that he hoped to never see them again. His mother and father watched as he walked down the road. They watched until they could no longer see him, and the tears rolled down their cheeks. They wondered, "What did we do wrong?"

Life must go on, and there was less stress around home without Sam's discouraging ways, yet they missed him. He was their son, and they loved him. Prayers with tears were poured out to their Heavenly Father every day for their missing son.

The New World
Chapter 5

Sam went down the road, topping the hill he looked back and saw his mother and father watching him. "Why are they watching me?" he mumbled. "I'm not changing my mind." With his head held high and his shoulders back he marched onward, thinking of how nice it was to be free from work and the authority of his parents.

After walking for a long time, he came to a little town, and he was hungry. He had walked close to twenty miles that day, so he stopped at a tavern where he ordered a sandwich. The waitress asked if he also wanted a beer. This kind of shocked him as his dad had never drank anything like that, and neither had he, but he told himself, "I'm free now, so why not?" Having never drunk anything so strong before, he didn't like it much. He kind of sipped away at the bitter tasting beer and did not want to drink it at all.

A young lady came into the tavern while he was eating. When she saw Sam sitting there alone she sat down beside him. "You're new here aren't you?" she asked him. Sam was taken back at having a stranger address him like that. "Yes, I just walked into town." he answered. The young lady continued the conversation, "Wow, you're sure good looking. Where do you live?" Sam looked around the smoky room as if he was looking for an answer, "I'm just traveling through to a land where there are pleasures a plenty." She said, "Where you going to spend the night? Why not come and spend the night with me?"

Sam slowly became aware of his surroundings as the sun broke through the window. His eyes were drawn to the young lady he had met the night before. He felt sick to his stomach and wanted to get out of there. The woman was still under the effects of the strong drink, so he slipped out without her knowing it. He was glad to get away from her and felt guilty for having yielded to her, but he forced his mind on to the pleasures that lay out ahead of him.

He hadn't gone far, when an automobile came along, which was something new to him. He knew they were out there, but at home they farmed with horses and used a buggy to go any distance. Most of the time, they walked. The vehicle stopped, and the man asked Sam where he was going. When he said he was going to see the pleasures of the world, the man told him, "You want to go to Chicago." Sam asked, "Where is that?" "It is a long way from here, but I'll take you as far as I'm going." The man replied. Sam got in and they went to a town that was much bigger than he ever thought there was. He liked the car, and asked about it, and where he can get one. The man told him they cost a lot of money, but Sam thought just maybe he could get one.

He asked the man if he would take him to where he got it. The man laughed, "No young man as you could buy one of these. However if you want to see them, I'll take you to where they are, but I want twenty dollars for taking you there. It is a ways out of my way." Sam just handed him twenty dollars, which surprised the man, but he took him to the dealer.

Sam was excited to see the automobiles and thought to have one would just be the most glorious thing a man could have. After talking to the salesman he decided to buy a new Ford Model T. He paid three hundred and thirty five dollars for it and he paid it with cash. The man asked how such a young man had so much money. He told him he had inherited it, so the salesman believed him. The salesman gave him some lessons on how to drive, and how to change a tire etc.

He thought, "Now this is the life." After a few days of learning to drive and what everything was for on the car, he headed on for Chicago. Soon he came into a town, where several people waved at him and wanted to talk to him, as not everyone had such a vehicle. He was very popular wherever he went with his Model T car. One day as he was traveling he heard a loud bang. The car veered to the left and then to the right. When he came to a stop, the left front tire was flat. He was glad he had been taught how to change a tire. When he got to the next town, he bought a new one. He ran out of gas one time, so he got a little gas can which he carried with him for such a time.

When he got to Indianapolis he found a group of boys who seemed so nice, and they just seemed to know where the most enjoyable places were. They really bragged him up, and told him he was really smart. They invited him into their gang, and they had some of the most interesting friends. They liked to party and had plenty of money. At night they would go to a tavern and play pool, and have a few drinks. He had never gotten to like the beer but being with them, and enjoying the things they did, he little by little acquired a taste for it. Sam being a natural with sports, soon got the hang of pool. He could beat most everyone. The boys were used to laying money on the game, and the winner took the kitty. Winning didn't make him liked, as he was taking their money, so he would buy them all beer, and whatever else they wanted, many times spending more than he had won.

Sam was the only one with a car, so the others would have him take them when they wanted to go places that was of any distance away. Sometimes they would pay for the gas, and sometimes not, but they always bragged on him and made him feel important. At times he would turn them down, especially when they wanted him to do something his dad had taught him was really bad, such as to go a way off, and steal and then use his car to get away quickly.

There was a party at one of the boy's home when his parents were out of town, and they invited a lot of their friends. Some of the friends lived a ways from the party, so he was asked to go get them. They told him they would have more fun if these people were there. So Sam agreed to go get them, and when he got there he was met by five girls, not too well dressed. At first he said, he would not take them, but they swayed him by asking if he really wanted to spoil the party. One put her arms around him and smiled at him, "You'll have fun if you take us." So he took them.

The party got carried away, and there was a lot of drinking. Not only did they drink all the beer that was purchased for the party, they drank what they found in the ice box. The boy, whose house they were in said his dad would be angry if they didn't replace it, so they ordered more and some extra. When it was delivered, they told the delivery guy that Sam would pay. When Sam refused, in their drunken state they threatened him if he wouldn't. Some said, "You're a good fellow" Two of the drunken girls went up to him and lovingly whispered into his ear, "You wouldn't betray us would you?" So he paid the bill. When he took the girls home he was stopped by the police for driving unsafely and was fined fifty dollars.

The next day, after the alcohol was out of his system, he was upset at what the party had cost him and said, "Never again." But it wasn't long until some of his friends came over and told him that he was the life of the party. So in a few weeks they again had a party, and he was again brought into it by flattery. Each time after it was over, and he had paid most of the bill, he would say he'd never do it again. Yet he would once again fall to the temptation for the fun he had, or at least thought he had. By and by his money was gone.

Then the time came when he didn't even have enough to pay his rent, so he was told to get out. One of his best friends, Rick, told him he could live with him, but his mother said, "Not for very long." Most of the people he thought were his friends forsook him when he couldn't pay for another party. Rick was the first boy he met when he came here, and had always been dependable. They were close friends.

Rick told Sam he had an uncle who lived just outside of Greenfield on a farm. He had a hog operation and hired people to work for him. If he got a job, maybe he could help them have more parties, as they were so much fun. Sam thought that if he would get more money, he still wanted to go to Chicago, where the real fun was, but for now his money was all gone.

Rick and Sam went to his uncle's farm just outside of Greenfield, and Rick introduced him to his Uncle George. George said he could use some help, but couldn't pay much, as there weren't good crops that year, because of the dry weather. He would give him a place to live, and some food, and a little wages.

Sam took the job, and moved in with a few of his things; however he left some things in the car. Since Rick needed a way back to Indianapolis Sam let him take his car. It was agreed that Rick would bring Sam's car back the next week. The car needed gas, so Sam gave him what little money he had left.

Later that week news arrived that Rick never made it home. Witnesses to the accident said it appeared the front right tire blew out and when the car veered to the right, the driver had overcorrected. The Model T had flipped over twice as it rolled down an embankment. The car was a total wreck and Rick had perished. When George told Sam about the accident he was very sad, both for his friend and his car.

George let him sleep in a room upstairs, but there was no heat up there. The cot he slept on was old and not a bit comfortable, but it was better than nothing. His apartment in Indianapolis had everything a person would want and he'd been used to life that way. Life had been really grand until he ran out of money. Now this!

George was a bachelor, and at fifty eight had never been married. He had inherited the home place a few years ago. Every morning he fixed oatmeal for breakfast. He let Sam have a little, but without milk or sugar. For dinner he could have a turnip, and supper an apple.

The work was hard and tiring. He realized he could not live long on what he was paid. Winter was upon them. He had to cut wood to have any heat at all in the house. There was a stove on the main floor, where George slept, and a wood fired kitchen stove, which took small pieces of wood. George expected him to cut and split all the wood, besides take care of the hogs. He got so hungry that he felt like he could eat the hog feed, but he knew that wouldn't be allowed.

He wanted to go someplace else, but he didn't know where. The cold winter winds blowing outside of his window helped convince him to stay until spring. One night as he lay there, shivering in his lumpy cot, he thought about his condition, and what he had done. It had been some time since he had a drink of beer, and he no longer desired it. He thought, "Why, my father's hired men always had all they wanted to eat and were happy. Why am I staying in this place?" He knew he wasn't worthy to be called his son, but if his father would only make him one of his farm hands.

The Homeward Trip
Chapter 6

Early in April, Sam gathered up his things and started on his way to his father's home back in Virginia. His time in Indianapolis had made him soft. He had not worked at anything strenuous during those two years. When he came to George's farm he was plenty pudgy, but now he had lost all that. The long winter and the hard work had toughened him up.

As he walked along the road he thought about it. He wondered if he was doing the right thing. His worldly friends had all forsaken him except his best friend, and he had died in the car accident. All his inheritance was gone. As the hours rolled by, he had plenty of time to think about the past few years, and what had transpired. This made him ashamed of himself.

The first day he went about fifteen miles, and his feet were getting sore. He came to a small stream of water, and sat on a log while soaking his feet in the cool bubbling stream. It felt relaxing to have the backpack off his back. As he sat there thinking, he happened to remember the little Bible that his dad had given him a long time ago. It was just a little one, but he had cherished it for many years. He got to thinking. He had taken it with him when he left home, but where was it? Looking through his bag, he decided it wasn't with him. Probably among the things in the car, and that was gone. The last thing he looked through was a small container, in which he kept some personal things, and there it was.

He leafed through it, and where it opened, he started to read. It caught his attention. It was where Jesus said, *"when an unclean spirit has gone out of a man, he walks in a dry place, and finds nothing, so he goes back where he had been, and finds it clean and empty. Then he goes and gets seven more spirits worse than himself, and they move into that person, so the last condition of that person is worse than the first.*" The chills ran down his back, as he thought, "The Lord is pointing out what would happen to me if I don't fill my life with the spirit of Jesus." Then he remembered a song his mother used to sing. Part of it went, "*Fill our hearts with thoughts of Jesus, and of Heaven where he has gone, and let nothing ever please us, He would grieve to look upon.*"

The more he thought about it, the more he was glad things didn't work out at George's. If George had money, and had paid him well, he may have gotten an accumulation of wealth, then have gone on to Chicago and fell into gangs worse than those in Indianapolis. He may never have come to the point of repentance. The thought made him chill.

The days were getting longer, but the mid April nights were still cold. He didn't have a tent, but he had gotten an old sleeping bag at a garage sale for only a few pennies. Even in its ragged shape he was always happy to crawl in for the night. He dreamed of his mother standing at the cook stove fixing breakfast, and oh what good things she was fixing.

He awoke to reality, but the dream gave him the determination to go on. He would bundle up his things and without any breakfast head onward toward home. As he walked he wondered how he could fill his thoughts with good things, so Satan wouldn't have any room to cause him to fall. Then he remembered a song, but only a part of it. It made him think of his condition, so he sang as best as he could as he walked along: "Jesus, thou art a sinner's friend, as such I look to thee, now in thy bowels of thy love, dear Lord remember me." With this the tears ran down his cheeks.

About ten o'clock that morning he came to a farm house, just as the farmer was coming out of the house to go to his work. He asked the farmer if there was anything he could do to get something to eat. He explained that he hadn't had anything to eat for over a day. The farmer, whose name was Eli, said if he would throw down hay from the mow to feed his cows, he'd see if his wife could fix him something.

Sam went to the barn and climbed up into the hay mow. Loosening the hay, he threw it down until Eli said it was enough. Sam said he would throw down enough for tomorrow if Eli wanted him to. Eli was pleased with Sam's willingness to go the extra mile. When they went to the house, Eli's wife Abigail had fixed him a plate of ham and eggs with fried potatoes. It was a delicious breakfast such as he had not seen for a long time. It was like the dream he had of his mother at the cook stove. When Abigail put the plate in front of him he bowed his head, and with the tears running down his cheeks, he offered the first prayer he had offered in years. It had been so long that he didn't know how to pray, only he prayed, "Thank you Lord." He ate part of his breakfast and asked if they cared if he took the rest with him. He had a long way to go, and he didn't have much money.

Sam thanked them for their hospitality. When he walked out the back door he noticed an ax sitting beside a pile of wood. He picked up the ax and split a nice size pile of wood for the kitchen stove. As he was about to leave, they asked him to come in; they wanted to talk to him. Eli said, "There are a lot of bums walking by these days wanting something to eat, but they don't want to work. You seem to be different, and we would like to know more about you."

Sam dropped his head, "I am a prodigal son of a good man and an angel of a mother." He then told them his story, and how he was now going home to try to become one of his father's hired men. After he told the story he looked up. They were both weeping. Then they told him about their son, their only son, who wanted to see the world. He had fallen among bad influences and was now living the life of the bad people. They hadn't heard from him in a long while, but were still praying for him.

They insisted he stay with them for a couple of days and rest his feet. He would then be more fortified to move on. Sam felt unworthy but submitted to their offer. That evening after the chores were done, Eli got the Bible, and read to them. He read about the lost sheep and the shepherd. Then he read the parable Jesus told of the prodigal son and Sam wept. He said he didn't expect to be treated like that if he ever got home. Then they all kneeled in prayer.

Sam helped Eli for the next two days. It made him think of how it was when he was a young boy at home. How good he had it. He wondered why their son left home, and then he remembered how it was with him. He was blinded by the allurements of Satan.

Sam and Eli were sitting on the porch swing watching the sunset. "Sam, why don't you stay over Sunday and go to church with us?"

Sam hung his head for a few moments then looked up at Eli. "Will they let a sinner as I am in the meeting house?"

Eli responded, "Jesus came into the world to save sinners."

Sam did stay and was much inspired with the love shown among the people. The singing was beautiful, and sermon was firm but kind. The preacher talked about Elijah being all alone up in the hills, at the mouth of a cave. The rocks rent, the tempest blew, yet he did not hear God. Then God came in a *still small voice.* The preacher said, "If you close your eyes and stop up your ears to the tempest of the world, and listen, you may hear the *still small voice of God.*"

That night as he was sleeping, he had another dream. In this dream, an angel stood at the foot of his bed and whispered, "Sam, God loves you. Be strong and I'll be with you, as long as you trust in the Lord."

Eli and Abigail gave Sam a good pair of shoes and a few other things a hiker needs. They would have liked to make an easier way of travel for him. They just didn't have the means. He told them he felt unworthy and if he had it too easy he might fall back into sin.

When he was ready to leave, they wanted to pray with him. They also prayed for their son and all others such as were in danger. It was then that he realized his parents must have been praying for him all this time. So they sent him on his way with their blessings.

As Sam's journey continued from town to town Satan tried to make him fall. People would offer to buy him a beer and girls would try to get him to stray from the path that was the way home. It was the picture of Eli and Abigail and their tears as they prayed for him and their son that gave him strength. The dream of his guardian angel reinforced his inward desire to walk with the Lord. He began to sing a song he remembered his parents singing. Although he didn't know it all, he would sing as much as he could. This helped to fill his mind of the good things of God and kept him going toward his father's house. He never passed up an opportunity to open his Bible and to read something, even if it wasn't but a sentence or two. At night he would read and pray. He had never realized how much encouragement there was in that little book, and it became his best friend along the journey.

Sam followed trails in the woods when they were not too far from the road. He enjoyed the forest, and the trails kept him away from the hobos along the roads. They weren't trustworthy and would steal if they had a chance.

One evening, in the hills of West Virginia, as the sun was about to set, he sat on a log, and read in his Bible. A feeling of peace swept over him and he began to sing *"Rock of ages, shelter me, let me hide myself in thee."* As he was finishing, *"When I take my fleeting breath, when my eyelids close in death,"* there was a snap of a twig which startled him. Turning around Sam saw an old man, walking with a cane and coming up the hill toward him. He stood up and said "Hello."

The old gent answered in a quavering voice, "Hello, I'm Joe. I live just down the hill a little. My wife, May is so sick, and when we heard the singing we thought the angels were coming to get us. I know you must be a Christian. We need some help. Would you help us until our son can get here? Oh my dear May is so sick."

Sam smiled, "Sure I will." Gathering up his things, he followed Joe down the hill. It wasn't far, and as they came to the little house, he heard someone calling out for Joe. As they entered the door, there was a pale little old woman on a couch. Joe introduced him to her, and said, "Sam is the one we heard singing."

In her weak voice, she said, "God bless you my son."

Joe asked Sam if he'd help him to give May some medicine, as he was too shaky. He said, "Oh, she needs it so bad." Joe got the medicine, which was a liquid in a bottle. Sam read the directions and helped her to sit up, and then he gave her the amount called for.

She said, "That will soon make me feel better."

Sam asked if she had eaten anything lately. Joe said, "No, we haven't had much since yesterday. We don't have any split wood for the kitchen stove, and I just can't handle the axe. When our son comes, or the church men, they'll split some for us."

Sam said he would split enough for them to have supper, and tomorrow morning he would split more. After splitting some wood, he started a fire in the stove, and asked Joe what he and May wanted him to fix. They wanted just a little chicken-noodle soup. Joe got a can of it out of the cupboard, and Sam fixed it for them. After a little prayer, Joe took a small bowl in to May. She was too weak to feed herself, so he tried to feed her. His hands shook so much, that he spilled some. Seeing the situation, Sam took the bowl from Joe and said he'd feed May. He told Joe that his soup was at the table and asked if he felt he could feed himself. Joe said he thought he could. Sam sat on the little chair, propped May up with some pillows, and slowly fed her. She said the soup tasted very good. She only ate about half of it, but it made her feel better.

Joe came in from the kitchen with a smile on his face and said, "That was sure good." He felt to get some hot food in him would help his shakiness. Sam felt they probably hadn't eaten right for a few days.

Joe asked Sam if he would read something out of the Bible to them. "My sight is so bad I can't read anymore. Could you please read the twenty third Psalm?"

As Sam read the familiar Psalm, May lay there with her eyes closed. Joe sat in the little rocker by her bed and held her hand. When Sam was done, May, in a *still small voice,* said, "Thank you. That is so comforting." She hesitated a bit, and then in a weak voice, asked, "Would you help us to sing the song we heard you singing in the woods?"

Sam said, "Sure."

Joe's quivery voice and May's weak one sang all the way through the song "Rock of Ages" with Sam, who tried not to be too loud. Just as they finished the last line, May fell off to a peaceful sleep.

"Our son lives a few miles away," Joe said, "but we have a Church family down the road just one mile. If they knew we needed help they would be glad to come. Would you mind going down there and telling them the situation?" Sam said he would be glad to, but as it was getting late, he would stay with them until the morning and then he'd go and tell them.

Sam looked at Joe, "Have you been getting the rest you need? You look tired."

"No," Joe replied, "I worry about ma, and I don't want to be asleep when she needs me. So I just sit in this rocker by her bed. When she needs something I'll be here, but, as of yesterday, I've got too shaky to give her the medicine." Sam said, "Joe, go into your room and go to bed. You need a good night's sleep. I'll sit here by May's bed and take care of her." Joe smiled, and after a simple but deep prayer he retired to his bed.

Joe had a good night, and May did too. She woke up once when it was time for her medicine, and Sam gave it to her. She soon went back to sleep. Joe was up once, but slept well. He felt much more rested, and didn't shake as much. May awoke a little later and had some sparkle in her eyes and a smile on her face. Sam started a fire in the cook stove. While Joe made some oatmeal, Sam toasted some bread. After Joe offered a touching prayer, he was about to take May's breakfast, when Sam said, "Let me feed May this morning, and by noon you may feel well enough to feed her.

Joe smiled, "Okay. Maybe by then she'll be able to come to the table."

After the dishes were done, and May was given her medicine, Sam went to the neighbors and told them about Joe and May's condition. He told them he intended to stay today, split more wood and help them all he could. The lady thanked him and said she would come soon. She did come and told them the ladies from church would bring food in and be available to help in any way. They would tell their husbands, so they would see that there was wood available. She apologized for not having checked on them. Joe said that they, being in their mid-eighties, probably should consider living with their son. They liked their little home, and church family, but when something like this happens, what should we do? May spoke up and said, "An angel sent Sam to help us." Sam turned his back as tears welled up in his eyes.

Sam split some wood that day and helped Joe with a few things he needed done. He told Joe he'd stay another night. The church family brought in a tasty dinner with enough for supper. May was getting some of her strength back and was able to sit at the table for a few minutes to eat, but soon lay back down.

That evening several of the young folks of their church family came over to sing. They knew Joe and May loved to sing. Sam recognized a lot of the songs and was able to sing along. Those he didn't know were beautiful. Little did they know, they were not only singing to an older couple, but to a forlorn and ship wrecked boy.

The next morning, May was feeling much better. Joe had a very good night and wasn't shaky. After having a hearty breakfast Joe wanted to have a farewell prayer. Then Sam bid them adieu. A girl from the church came to help out for the day.

As he climbed back up the hill to where he was when Joe came to him two nights ago, he thought of what happened those two days. He felt he had received more than he gave. He felt his soul was full. He stood by the log where he had been sitting, and, although he couldn't see Joe and May's cottage, he knew they could hear him as he started singing, *"My friends, I bid you all adieu, I leave you in God's care. If I here no more see you go on I'll meet you there."*

Five months after leaving George's farm he was finally getting close to home. That is when Sam started having a feeling of anxiety. Satan started putting doubts in his mind. He said, "They will drive you away like you are a bandit. Your Mother has died, and your dad has married another woman. She will call the police and have you put in jail. When your brother sees you coming he will shoot you. You better come with me and have the fun you deserve."

There were other things Satan tried to tell him, but then Sam remembered the dream of the angel, and the love and prayers of Eli and Abigail. He thought of his experience with Joe and May. Sam fell upon the ground and poured out his heart unto the Lord. Then it seemed he felt a hand on his shoulder. This made him think of what he read about Jesus in the garden and the sin of the whole world was on his shoulders. Then the angels came and ministered unto him.

With faith and determination Sam went onward. As he topped the hill that led down to the home place, he stopped and stood there for a long time. He prayed for his mother and father and for John, and he thanked the Heavenly Father who sent an angel to lead him home.

The Reunion
Chapter 7

It took faith to go onward, but Sam knew this was what he wanted to do, so he continued. The first person he saw was his mother going into the house. The sight of her caused him to break down and weep. He stood there a while weeping. When he regained his composure, he moved onward. His eyes fell on his father standing beside the barn looking his way. It was as if he had been looking for him ever since he left home. As Sam came closer his father acted as if he had seen a vision and started running toward him.

As he got to him, Sam hung his head in humility, "I have sinned against Heaven and in your sight. I am no more worthy to be called your son, please make me as one of your hired men." He hoped his father would not send him away. His dad threw his arms around him and wept. Amos took Sam to the house, where his mother could not believe her eyes. She began to weep as she embraced her son.

Amos called the family and the neighbors together for a reunion to celebrate his son's return home. Alice opened some canned beef and made mashed potatoes and noodles. The neighbors brought in food, ice tea, and a lot of desserts. After they embraced, wept, and laughed, Sam, being so over-whelmed with the welcome home, asked if they would sing some good old songs of Zion. The ones they used to sing when he was a small boy. He didn't tell them at that time, but it was these songs which helped to fill his inner being with the Spirit of the Lord along his way back home.

They got the song books out and started to sing, and did they ever sing. As his mother started to sing she noticed Sam singing with enthusiasm, she couldn't help but weep for joy.

John had been working in the fields all day and was tired. He came in just as they began to sing. He was surprised to see so much activity at the house and then to hear the singing. He asked one of the farm hands what this was all about. He was told that Sam had come home and their father was having friends and family over to celebrate.

This made John angry, and he told the farm hand he would not go in. The farm hand went to the porch, and motioned for Amos to come out. He told him what John had said, so Amos went out and talked to him. John was the angriest Amos had ever seen him. John said, "I've served you all these years, and you have never given me a party like this. Now, when your youngest son who wasted your money on riotous living has come home you celebrate."

Amos replied, "Son, son, you know that all that I have is yours. It is true you have never disobeyed your mother or me. You are as dependable as can be. It is true your brother spent his inheritance on wild unclean living, and is now financially broke. He had been in a lost condition with the Lord, and had gotten as low as could be. When he was hungry and cold, his worldly friends forsook him. Then he came to himself and remembered his father's house, but he felt unworthy to come home."

"It was only by encouragement from some good godly people that he made the effort to return. Son, it was really hard for him to come home. When he came to me, he confessed he had sinned against God and me. He felt he was not worthy to be called my son. John, I understand how you feel, but let's think about the Scripture where Jesus told about the sheep which had gone astray, and how the shepherd left the ninety-nine and went into the wilderness and found the one who went astray. John, what did he do when he found that one?"

John thought for a little and said, "He rejoiced more of that one, than of the ninety-nine that went not astray."

"That's right," Amos responded. "Now son, do you think he didn't like the ninety-nine? Of course he loved them. They were faithful and could be depended on. The one that went astray was in danger of being killed by a fox or lion, whereas the ninety-nine were safe under the shepherd's care."

"John, your brother went astray, and was in the wilderness of the wolves and lions. Satan had gotten a hold of him, and had intentions of killing him. His soul was in a lost condition, and he may never have found his way back, had it not been for the prayers of those who cared about him. John, you have been the ninety-nine to Mother and me. We do love you, and we need to forgive your brother."

"John, it is not about money, or farms, you know we gave this farm to you when Sam got his inheritance, and it will be yours. This is about lost souls. Remember the story you boys used to like about Joseph and how mean his brothers treated him? How that Joseph forgave them? John, he was a type of Jesus, and we know Jesus has forgiven us of all our sins, and we want to forgive Sam. He has repented and there is in him a new spirit. If you can forgive him and talk with him, I think you will be glad. He is as a lost sheep that has been found."

John, having always obeyed his Father, said that he would try, but first he had to go the barn. Amos watched his son as he went into the barn, and soon he came out with a little lamb in his arms. Amos asked, "Son, why do you have one of your lambs?" John answered, "This is a ewe lamb of my best sheep, and I'll not go in without a gift. I want to give Sam this ewe lamb as a new start, so he can someday have his own flock that will hear his voice." Tears ran down Amos' face.

The sun had set as they made their way to the house. The evening was calm, and the stars were bright. When they got to the porch, Sam saw them coming with a lamb, so he went out on the porch. John said, "Sam, I forgive you of all that you have done. From the best of my flock, I'm giving you this ewe lamb for a new start. I pray that someday you may have a large flock of sheep that will hear your voice."

They threw their arms around each other and wept. Out of the windows the music of the singing was beautiful.

Blessed assurance, Jesus is mine, and oh the foretaste of glory divine.

Heir of salvation, Purchase of God, born of his Spirit, washed in his blood.

This is my story, this is my song, Praising my Savior all the day long,

This is my story; this is my song, praising my Savior all the long.

The brothers stood facing each other and holding hands with tears rolling down their cheeks. Beside them stood Amos and Alice holding onto each other, with tears flowing. This was the day they had been praying for. The boys walked into the house side by side, with the lamb in Sam's arms. In his heart was *the Lamb of God that takes away the sin of the world*, as well as in the hearts of everyone there. Amos and Alice followed them as someone started singing.

Blest be the tie that binds our hearts in Christian love,
The fellowship of kindred minds is like to that above.

Time for a Change
Chapter 8

It was getting late when the last people left. Amos and Alice wanted to talk to Sam, but being so late, they told him to go up to his room and go to bed. They said to rest as long as he wanted. They could talk some other time.

As Sam went up the stairs, he thought about the time he wanted to get away from here. Now he felt he was an intruder to even be in this house, let alone sleeping in the room that used to be so familiar to him. He closed the door and looked around. Everything was as he left it close to three years ago. On the stand by his bed was the Bible his parents gave him when he graduated from the eighth grade. On the chest of drawers was his song book, and beside it was his Sunday hat. He opened a drawer and there were several of his clothes all folded up in the manner Mom always did. He noticed there wasn't any dust on things, and he wondered if she went up there regularly to dust.

The covers on the bed were the same ones he used while still at home. As he turned them back, he saw a note on the pillow. He picked it up, and in his mother's handwriting was this note: *Son, if you ever come home I want you to know the Lord still loves you, and I do too, Mom.* He sat on the bed with the note held tight against his breast, and sobbed for a long while.

Sam didn't wake up until about noon the next day. When he awoke, the note was still clenched in his hand. He picked up his Bible and turned to the first Psalm and carefully read it. Then he knelt beside his bed and prayed.

He went downstairs and found his mother at the kitchen stove fixing dinner. Immediately the dream he'd had, as he slept by the stream flashed through his mind. His mother turned around and said, with a smile, "Good morning."

"Good morning!" Sam replied, "I feel like I have been lazy."

Alice explained that they could tell he was very tired and thought he should get some rest. "That was the best bed I've had for a long time," Sam said as he opened the note and came to her, putting a kiss on his mother's cheek. "Thank you, Mother," he whispered as he shed some tears. Alice kept her back to him as she worked at the stove but wiped tears from her eyes with her apron.

Amos and John came in as Sam and his mother were putting the last things on the table. They both greeted Sam as they washed up. They all sat down and bowed their heads while Amos prayed. He had trouble at times keeping his composure, but he had an appropriate prayer for the occasion. No longer did he have to pray for the empty place at the table. As they ate they tried to act as if nothing was unusual. Amos and John talked about the morning's work and what they planned to do in the afternoon. Sam was quiet as he still felt he was an intruder, but there wasn't anything said about him. He noticed he wasn't included in their afternoon planning. Before they went out Amos turned to Sam and said, "Son, we think you should spend some time with your mother, at least a week or more. Then we'll talk about the work."

Sam liked the way his father said, "Son".

He wondered what he could do for her. He remembered the times they worked in the garden together and the times they made candy. It seemed it was easier to talk to her than his father, although that wasn't difficult.

Alice said, "Son, would you want to help me pick some apples this afternoon?"

"Sure," Sam replied, "I'll get the baskets."

His mother asked him to get two of them. They had an enjoyable time picking apples, and soon both baskets were full. "Shall I get more?" Sam asked.

"No," his mother answered, "I think this is enough, but I do want you to help me make some apple sauce out of these."

They spent an enjoyable afternoon visiting as they peeled and cored apples. Alice said, "Son, there is just the two of us here. Would you like to tell me about your life since you left home?"

Sam hesitated a little before telling her the whole story. Sometimes he would shed some tears and she would too. When he told her about the little Bible his father gave him, about Eli and Abigail, and about Joe and May she had to stop and wipe her eyes.

Sam and his mother worked together the whole week. He would tell her things she wanted to know. She also filled him in on things that had happened while he was gone. They got the apples all canned and the garden cleaned off for winter. He confessed he was ashamed of what he had done, and how he had wasted their money foolishly. She comforted Sam by explaining to him that although the money was gone, he wasn't. He could use his life for the Lord's work. She encouraged him to search the Bible to see what was expected of him.

The evening devotions were as before, but now he enjoyed them and would ask questions. Mornings were also an inspiration. He needed those blessings to help fill his life with the good things that keep out the devil.

They were now including Sam in the daily planning and he was made to feel a part of the farm, although as a hired hand.

Uncle Ronald's came over one day and Enos was along. He had become a member of the Church and wanted to talk to Sam. He said he was glad Sam had come home and was reading his Bible, but felt to come part way and not to be baptized was not letting the Lord all the way into his heart. He said, fact is to be forgiven by God, we must be born again.

He said, "It takes faith, which you have, repentance, which you have, and baptism which is a washing away of your sins, which you have not done." Enos told Sam, "Look it up in Acts, second chapter. Peter was speaking on the day of Pentecost when he told the people to, *Repent and be baptized every one of you in the name of the Jesus Christ for the remission of sins and ye shall receive the gift of the Holy Ghost."* Enos continued, "Unless you are born again, Satan will have an advantage over you. Your father, mother, and John have forgiven you, but what about God?" He told Sam about things he had done as a teenager for which he was now ashamed, "But by the cleansing blood of the Lamb of God through water baptism, I am forgiven. Now I walk in the new way of life. When you are baptized you make promises to God. Afterwards, the Minister will lay hands on you and pray that all your sins will be forgiven, that your name will be written in the Lambs' Book of Life, and you will receive the indwelling of the Holy Spirit. You need this."

Sam, looking out across the rolling hills, pondered what Enos had been telling him. He had been reading his Bible and was very familiar with the verses Enos mentioned. Looking back at Enos he replied, "I have been trying to fill my heart with the love of God, but hadn't thought much about baptism. You are right Enos, as a believer and a follower of Jesus I need to be baptized."

That evening Sam talked to his parents about his decision. Amos read the third chapter of St. John and they discussed it. Sam told the family, "I remember when John was baptized. At that time, I thought I would someday do the same, even though I soon forgot. Now I am ready."

Amos said, "Tomorrow we'll go over to the Elder and tell him".

The next day, when they talked to the Elder he told them there were others to be baptized the next Sunday as well. He encouraged Sam to spend much time praying and reading the

Bible. "It is a lifetime commitment, which is not to be broken," he said. "Be sure to count the cost."

The New Plan
Chapter 9

"Today is a special day," Sam thought as he arose early and did his morning chores. He told his mother he didn't want any breakfast as he was so excited. It was the day he anticipated. There were five to be baptized today, and he was one of them.

The service was very impressive. He felt closer to the Lord than he ever had. The minister was very kind and covered all the questions thoroughly. He explained the importance of faithfulness to the vows we make to our God. He told not only the applicants, but also all those in attendance, "Walking the new way of life is a joy when we have our hearts right with the Lord."

Now that Sam was a member of the church he felt he had more of a responsibility to be a light in this world to the Lord. This helped him to be fortified against the wiles of the devil. He read in The Revelations about the seven Churches of Asia who were given an opportunity to overcome and the blessings which could be theirs.

Sam was so grateful for the privilege of being a part of a loving, God fearing family. He loved to sing. One of his special songs was *Jesus, lover of my soul, let me to thy bosom fly.*

John and Sam enjoyed each other more than ever before. It was so comforting to be forgiven from all the sins of his past, by his family and by God.

Sam had been home for six weeks when dad gave him a job as a hired hand. It was corn husking time and Sam was to take the same wagon he and his dad had used to help an injured neighbor years ago. One of the other farm hands had to show Sam how to harness the team. With the horses hitched to the box wagon, he headed for the field. Sam wondered if he could remember how to use the husking knife. He thought about how fast time goes by as he looked down at the worn knife beside him on the wagon. "This is yours now, son. I'm just getting too old to be husking corn anymore," Amos had said when he had handed it to Sam.

He noticed how the horse next to the standing corn tried often to get an ear, but like he had been taught, he had put on the muzzle correctly, which prevented the horse from doing so. Sam remembered what his dad told him about the little boy and the candy dish, and thought of the wisdom of his father.

Sam worked hard, but his wrist wasn't used to this manner of exercise. By the end of the day he had husked a little less than one load. His arms were so tired and it was disappointing not to do more. He remembered how he had helped his dad do two loads in a day and even unloaded them. That was back when he was a young boy. Sam felt he was already a failure. When he went in, he apologized to his dad for not doing more. His dad said, "It takes time to toughen the arm muscles. By the time the season is over, you will see a difference."

John had a special friend Mary, and there were indications of a wedding in the future. He, being of a quiet nature, didn't talk about it openly. He had some talks with his mother at times, but she kept everything confidential.

One evening after the chores were done, Amos and Sam were talking about John and Mary. Amos said the couple would like to get married the following September, but they didn't know where to live. Amos said, "You know I gave this farm to your brother, but he doesn't want to make us leave."

Sam thought about it for a moment then said, "What about building a house onto the corner of the main house that would be big enough for you and mother?"

"But what would you do?" Amos replied. Sam said, "I've been thinking about it for awhile. I noticed how much John and Mary seem to like each other and realized it may be the will of God they marry. I believe she would be a wonderful addition to our family. Her family are good pillars in the Church, and I want to wish them God's blessings. I believe after we get the corn husked this fall, I could take a couple of the hired hands back into the woods, and we could fall enough timber to build you and mother a nice house onto this one if John and Mary feel it okay."

"As for me," Sam continued, "I think I can find a place to live. You and mother have been so good to me even when I didn't deserve it. I do appreciate all you have done. I've been thinking I would like to get into the building business. Ever since I helped the brethren rebuild Otis Yoder's house, after the fire, I feel like that may be my calling. I would like to build you and mother a house, and would consider it an honor if you feel to let me do it."

Sam's ideas gave Amos something to think about. He talked to Alice that night, and asked that she think about it for awhile. The next day, she said she didn't sleep well. She was thinking about moving from their home, which they had lived in for so many years. "Time does move on, and we are getting older, so maybe it is time for us to down size. A smaller home would make less work for me, but I think we should talk to John and Mary and get their input on it." That sounded like a good idea to Amos.

A couple of days later Amos and John were working together and Amos mentioned Sam's idea. John, being a quiet sort of person, didn't say anything for awhile. They were loading manure into the spreader, one on each side. After awhile John said, "That would be nice, but I don't want to do anything to cause a rift in our family. Sam has been enjoyable to be around, ever since he turned his life over to the Lord. I would not want to cause him to back slide."

"That is true," Amos replied. "I appreciate your concern, but that should not be a problem considering it was Sam's idea. I have noticed how much he has grown in the faith of the Lord."

"Yes, I also noticed that, and it helps me in my spiritual life as well," John said.

Amos asked, "Would it be alright if we had Mary and her parents over some evening to discuss it?"

John leaned on the handle of his pitchfork, thinking for a moment. "Let me mention it to Mary, and if it is alright with her we can do that. Of course we'll want to pray about it."

Sunday after the singing, on the way home, John mentioned it to Mary. She was silent for a couple of minutes before answering her soon to be husband. "I think it's a good idea for our families to get together to discuss it."

Alice invited Mary's parents, Joseph and Elizabeth to come for supper one evening. After supper and the dishes were done, they gathered in the living room around the heating stove. After a little small talk, Amos opened the subject. He said he and Alice had thought about it for a while, and they felt it was time for them to down size.

Joseph said Mary had mentioned it to them. He suggested they kneel in prayer, before they discuss it. They all knelt while he offered a touching prayer. After prayer, Amos suggested Sam tell them his offer. After Sam finished, John expressed his concerns about his parents moving to a smaller home. Amos explained that, after thinking on it for a while, they felt if it was in the hearts of their sons, they would be happy with the plan. Joseph and Elizabeth said they could give their blessings on the plan, provided it was pleasing to John and Mary. John looked at Mary who smiled back at him. "We have prayed about it," John said, "and feel we are blessed to have this opportunity."

Alice sat there with tears falling down her cheeks, "Godly love is so beautiful."

Once the leaves had dropped in October, Amos and the boys went to the woods to mark trees which were ready for harvest. There were more of them than Amos was aware of. They marked several poplar and oak trees. They even found a few ash and red elms.

The fall weather was exceptionally nice, and by the end of November the corn was all husked and in the cribs. The Wagoner boys even had time to help a neighbor with his corn. Having had such nice weather, and the harvesting being complete, Amos said the hired men could help with the falling of the trees.

It was the first week of December when Sam, with a couple of the hands, went to the woods. The light snow the night before made for a beautiful day. The temperature had dropped to twenty-five degrees, but with no wind it made for a perfect day to fall trees.

By evening they fell three trees. One was an ash and the other two poplars. Sam was very tired, but he was so happy. When he told his dad how many they got down, Amos was pleased, "Son, those muscles have toughened up since the first day of corn husking, haven't they?" Sam smiled.

The next morning John rode over to the sawmill to see if the sawyers had time to mill their logs. They told him to start bringing them in the following week. When that day came they had several cut down and ready. More snow was on the ground, so they were able to put the wagon bed on the sled for hauling logs. By using the largest team, they were able to take two logs at a time over the snow. Doing it with the sled, which was lower to the ground than a wheeled wagon, made it easier to load. They placed chains down across the wagon bed and out onto the ground, then rolled the logs onto the chains. Putting the chains across the logs, and hitching the team to the chains, they would roll the logs onto the wagon.

After a few trips to the mill some of the earlier logs were sawn, and they were able to bring a load of lumber back with each trip. They put the lumber in stacks, with one inch strips between the boards, to let them dry.

Sam got so enthused with cutting trees and the pile of lumber growing, that he had trouble stopping in time to do the chores in the evening. Sometimes he was so tired, he wouldn't eat much supper and then would fall asleep during evening devotions. Amos talked to him about how Satan doesn't care how he lures us away from the Lord. "I believe we should take a week off from the woods. Work is fine, if we don't make it our god." Sam dropped his head, "Thank you dad. I was getting too enthused and was slipping from my Bible reading time and meditations."

Amos and Alice talked about how it is so easy to get involved in carnal things to the point we lose sight of the Spiritual. Alice said she heard that Ronald and Sarah were struggling to keep up with their work and were low on wood for their stove. She asked Amos if they could leave the hired men in charge of the chores for two or three days and go see them. "We could help them to catch up," she explained.

Amos asked the boys what they thought, and they were delighted to go. Sam said "The men have been working hard. I think we should reduce their workload to only the daily chores while we're gone. We could let them have the rest of the time off to be with their families."

Amos liked that idea and made those arrangements with the hired hands. He told them they would still get their full pay. They were happy to oblige, so it was decided to leave the next day for Uncle Ronald's. When they got there, Ronald's were delighted to see them. After their greetings, they brought their things in, and the boys went to the barn to help Enos with his chores. The next day Ronald and Sarah's daughter Joyce Garber arrived with her husband, Henry, and their three month old son, Adam. Sam was disappointed his other cousin, Thomas, was away working for a friend in Ohio. The families spent three delightful days working together, visiting, engaging in scriptural talk, and praising God.

The New Home
Chapter 10

The logging went well, and by the first of January more than enough logs had been cut to build the addition. Sam took his father's advice seriously and only worked six hour days. It seemed they still got about as much done in a week and weren't nearly as tired. This gave them time to spend doing other things and more time for reading the Bible.

There were some January days when the weather was too stormy to do anything but the chores. Regardless of the adverse weather, they did get all the logs moved to the Sawmill. The mill shut down during the colder days, so it was March before they got all their lumber home.

With all the trees they fell, there were a lot of tops to work up. Sam felt they should try to get them cut into buzz poles as they had time, so he and some of the hired men found themselves back in the woods most days when weather permitted. John helped when he could, but he took over the cattle and the sheep, in order to let Sam free to work the woods. Amos told Alice one day, after listening to the boys discussing the work, "It sure is nice to see the co-operating spirit that is in our boys." Alice looked at him and smiled.

April arrived and brought with it warmer days. The tree tops were all worked up and cut into fire wood. Sam was anxious to get started on the house. They had spent some time as a family discussing the plans. John thought he wanted to have a basement, especially since it could be a walk out. He said there were plenty of stones in the stone pile to lay up the walls. It didn't matter to Amos and Alice, but they felt it would likely be helpful for John and his family. Sam assured the family that it was fine with him, if that was what they wanted.

Before it got fit to work in the fields, Sam took one of the teams, and the slip scoop and started to dig the basement. John had talked to one of the neighbors who had another slip scoop they could use. With another team and scoop they were really digging out the dirt. When it came chore time, Amos came with another team, and took Sam's place. Working the slip scoop was hard work, but Amos thought he could do it for awhile. John let his team rest while he was doing his chores. With a rested team John was soon moving dirt again. One day a neighbor showed up with his team and helped out. Because of the consistent hard work, the basement was dug in two weeks. Amos said, "Working together sure gets a big job done."

With the help of the hired men, and anyone who had time, they soon had the footing concreted. Next was the task of laying the rock walls. It was getting time to work in the fields. It was decided that Sam, along with one of the hired hands would lay up the wall while John and the others would work the fields. Amos felt he could do some things, and Alice said she would try to keep the workers supplied with ice tea or lemonade.

"This is just like the wagon no longer stuck in the mud," remarked Sam.

John looked at him and said, "Dad sure gave us some good illustrations of the way to get things done."

It took a lot of perseverance, but by the first week of July, the basement's walls were all laid up, and the house was ready to frame.

Several of the Church members said they wanted to help when they raised the building, so Sam set a day. So many came to help that it was hard to get to do much. The women brought break and dinner. By noon the rafters were up, and part of the sheeting was on.

When the call came for dinner, the men all took turns around the old wash tub. Once the morning grime was washed away Amos, John, and Sam all thanked those who were so generous as to leave their work to come and help. Uncle Ronald offered a prayer for the food and for the privilege of brethren working together. Sam felt he was the one who benefited the most, but he remembered how blessed he felt when he went to a working and worked with other brethren for a cause.

They enjoyed a delicious meal and were soon back to work. The sound of hammers echoed throughout the farm, and by the time the sun was low in the west the roof was on and the doors and windows in. As the last of the brethren left to go do chores, the Wagoner family sat down on the dwindling pile of lumber. In the waning light, they looked in amazement at what had been accomplished. What a wonderful blessed day.

Sam and John worked together on trimming the house. They spent evenings in the shop making beautiful cupboards for their mother and some nice fruit shelves for the basement. John spent as much time as he could on the house, but the farm took priority. He told Sam to concentrate on the addition and not worry about his chores. The work went well, and by the second week of August, the addition was complete. Sam thought porch swings would enhance the porches, so he built two: one for John's and one for his parents.

Alice was very happy with her new house and anxious to move in. Moving day was scheduled for the first day of September. Some of the neighbors and church members came to help. By noon Amos and Alice were in their new home. There was a door between the two houses, but Amos' would use the door on their porch to enter their home.

Once the main house had been cleaned out, John and Mary, along with her folks, did a walk through. They wanted to see if anything needed to be done before the wedding. Mary told John, "Your mother was such a good house keeper. I don't see anything that needs done."

The ladies said, "Yes, it is clean, but while we are here, let's give it a thorough cleaning anyway." Alice thought that was a good idea, so that afternoon it got a good going over.

The neighbor they had helped husk his corn the previous fall wanted to talk to Sam. He and Sam withdrew to the side a little, and he said, "Sam, I've been thinking about you. I have noticed the Christian Spirit you seem to possess. I know you will need someplace to live when John and Mary get married. My house seems so big and lonely ever since my wife Mabel passed away. I so much appreciate you helping husk my corn last fall. That gave me time to be with Mabel in her last days. Sam, would you consider moving in with me, at least for awhile?"

"Thank you for the offer," Sam answered. "I've been praying the Lord would open a door for me. This may be it; however, I want to talk to my parents first."

When Sam told his parents about the offer, a smile came over both of their faces. Alice let a tear trickle down her cheek. Amos said, "Josh is surely lonely since Mabel passed away. He is a good brother in the Church, and I believe you may be a help to him, and he may be to you." Sam talked to John about it, and he was all smiles. The next day, Sam went over to see Josh, and they agreed on terms. So three days before John and Mary's wedding Sam moved in with Josh.

The wedding day came, and along with it there was a lot of family to keep. John and Mary said they could bed a few guests and Amos' were able to bed one family. Josh told Sam he thought they could keep a family or two. Sam said his bedroom was available. He would sleep in a sleeping bag on the floor.

The service was plain, but nice. Uncle Ronald married them. He talked about the most important events in a person's life. He said, "The most important relationship is with God by Christian baptism. The next is the marriage vows. They are both made before God and are not to be broken by man." He had a lot of good counsel to the groom, and to the bride. One of the things he emphasized was true faithful love and having a forgiving heart. As usual, there were some tears shed, but it was a happy occasion. Another new godly home was formed.

Trials and Joy
Chapter 11

Sam was enjoying his new home. Josh was a deep spiritual man, which helped Sam's closeness to the Lord continue. Sam would often walk over to see his mother and father. One day Josh hinted it would be nice if he had a porch swing. On his seventy-fifth birthday, Josh stepped out on the porch and there hung a swing. "Why, I wonder how that got there," he quizzed Sam. "I believe I'll fix you an extra egg for breakfast." Sam looked at him and smiled. Sam always made sure there was plenty wood of split for the kitchen stove and, in cold weather, plenty of wood for heating. He didn't neglect his folks along these lines either.

Two years rolled by and Sam's reputation as a carpenter had spread. He had a long list of customers waiting to have their projects built. With less time to work on the farm, he was afraid John would be resentful, so he decided it was time to have a talk with his dad and John. One evening he went to his parent's home and told his dad the three of them needed to discuss his situation. Amos said, "Come in and have a chair, I'll go see if John can come over." Amos returned and explained that John's were just finishing supper and would be right over. Soon John and Mary with their little Susie soon came. Sam liked to tickle his little niece. He loved to see her smile.

Sam brought up the subject that was on his mind. He told them he was enjoying carpentry work and believed he could keep busy, but he didn't want to cause them to be short handed on the farm. Amos spoke up and said that he and mother were bowing out of the farming, as they are older, and the farm was John and Mary's. "We feel to have a small pasture with a few sheep and a little plot for a little garden."

John said, "Sam, you have been such a good brother ever since you turned your life over to the Lord and were baptized.

You and I have worked together for about three years now, and I've enjoyed every minute of it. Time does change things. The opportunity of being a carpenter and having your own crew, may be the new start the Lord is giving you financially. The best decision you made was when you chose to walk with the Lord. Now He is making a way for you in your occupation. I may cut back a little on the farming. If not, I can get more hands. Mary and I wish you God's blessings. If you ever need us we're here."

Sam thanked them and asked if they could have a family prayer together. They all bowed and Amos led them in a tearful prayer.

Sam was busy, and he hired some young boys to work for him part time. He built a house for some folks in town. Then he built a garage for their neighbors. The work seemed to come naturally for him. He also built a small utility shed at Josh's to have a place to make cabinets.

The time came when work was slack, and he remembered Joe and May Lentz over in Jeffrey, West Virginia. He told Josh one evening he would like to go over there and see if they were still alive. When Josh heard where Sam wanted to go, he told him he would like to go along, as he also knew some folks in those parts. "We can take Fred, he is a younger horse and worthy for a trip like that."

Sam went over to his folks and told them what they were planning to do. Amos volunteered to do Josh's chores and look after the place while they were gone. Then he said, "Watch for the dangers along the way."

Soon after breakfast and the devotions, they were on their way. Josh wasn't used to the way of roughing it, so they took a tent and plenty of covers. They also loaded the wagon with plenty of food and water for them and the horse. In the evening before it turned dark, they would set up camp and build a fire. As they cooked supper over the fire, Sam explained, "This is really modern compared to how I did it going the other way a few years ago."

Josh would always thank the Lord for the food and for the protection along the way. He seemed to enjoy the trip, except for the hard ground. "This isn't as comfortable as my bed at home." Josh mumbled.

After a few days they came to the church where Joe and May attended. Sam said they were about to Joe's place. When the house came in sight, they could see someone on the front porch. Sam told Josh to stop. He wanted to walk the rest of the way. They tied the horse to a tree, and then climbed a little way to a trail. Sam said, "This trail means something special to me, I'll explain later." They walked to where the log was behind Joe's house. It was still there, but had rotted a little. "It was from here I sang *Rock of Ages* when I was on my way home. Joe heard me and came up to see who was singing. Now I want to sing it again." He and Josh sang the familiar song, and by the time they were done, they spotted Joe walking up the hill with his cane.

It had been a few years and Joe didn't recognize Sam at first, but as soon as Sam smiled, he remembered. They embraced and wept on each other. Sam introduced Joe and Josh. Joe motioned the others to follow, "Come on down, ma will be glad to see you."

When they entered the house, May, who had been lying on the couch, sat up, "Surely it is our angel." She grabbed his hand and would hardly let go. Sam introduced her to Josh. She shared with him, "One time a few years ago, I was very sick, and Sam's angel sent him to help us." Then Sam told Josh the story of that day.

Joe said, "Sit down and have some tea."

"We have a horse and buggy just down the road a bit," Sam explained. "I'll run and get them, and then we'll sit and visit." Soon he was back, tied the horse to a post, then came in and sat down.

Joe said, "Sam, the day you left we were shedding some tears, when we heard you singing, *My friends I bid you all adieu,* then the tears really flowed. We are so glad to see you again." They all had a lot of things to talk about. Joe continued, "The girl that came to help the day you left, has been coming to help us ever since. Her name is Martha Jones. She is such a nice girl, and is such a help. If we need wood cut or split, she tells her dad, and he comes to do it. The church people are so good to care for the old and needy."

It wasn't long before Martha came, and then Sam remembered her. She was one of the young folks that sang that night when he was there a long time ago.

Josh asked Joe about some of his family and friends who lived in the area. Joe knew them and said several of them attend his church. He said, "If you would like, we can go visit some of them tomorrow." Josh was delighted to hear that. Joe invited them to stay for supper and spend the night.

As Joe was fixing supper, he said, "Sam, do you remember the supper you fixed for us of chicken and noodle soup the night we were so sick?"

Sam said, "I remember it very vividly. I am glad to see you two in good health now."

Martha was cleaning the house, and when she was done, she said, "May, being you have company I'll not stay for supper as I usually do, but I'll be back in the morning to do the dishes."

"Oh, we'd be disappointed if you don't stay. Please stay." May replied.

Martha went to the kitchen and told Joe, "You visit with your friends while I finish getting supper."

Joe gave her a smile and said, "Okay, if you need me say so."

Soon Martha called them to the table. When they all sat down, Joe thanked them for coming, and asked Josh to offer thanks for the blessings they had. As Josh offered a very grateful prayer, Sam sat there with tears slipping down his cheeks. He couldn't help to think about the condition of Joe and May, and himself the last time he was seated at this table. Yes, they were all so blessed.

After a simple but nourishing meal, Joe and Josh retired to the living room. Martha and May proceeded to clean up the table and wash the dishes. Sam told May, "You are much better than the last time we ate here, but I want to help again. Why don't you go and sit in your chair?"

She looked up at him and said, "Sam, you are like a son to us. Do you care if we call you son?"

He smiled at her and answered, "If you like." Martha washed the dishes and Sam dried as they sang some of the good ol' songs of Zion.

Martha stayed until after devotions, then told them good night and went home. After she left, May looked at Sam with a twinkle in her eye and said, "Martha is such a sweet girl."

After turning in for the night it wasn't long until Sam heard Josh snoring. He knew he was tired, but Sam had trouble sleeping. He thought of the night he sat up with May so Joe could get some much needed sleep. He thought of all that had transpired since that night. Then he thought of the enjoyment of helping do the dishes as he and Martha sang. Could it be that the Lord is bringing him and Martha together?

After breakfast the men went to see some of Josh's old friends. Some of them were his cousins he hadn't seen for a long while. They took lunch with an older couple who was a cousin of Josh's wife, Mabel.

Soon after lunch, Joe said he thought he ought to go and check on May, as she didn't feel to go along. Sam said, "I'll go, so you and Josh can continue to visit other places. I can run there in a little while. You take the buggy. Maybe I can read to her." Joe said, "She'll like that." When Sam made it to the house, May had just laid down to rest. She was glad to see him, as she was concerned about Joe. Sam thought it amazing how older couples have so much feeling for each other. Sam told her Joe and Josh were having a good day. They each knew the people they visited and had much to talk about. "They likely will be home before long." he said, adding, "Would you like me to read something to you?"

May wanted the thirty-forth Psalm read. Once Sam finished he told May, "There is so much in this Psalm, but what stood out to me the most is the fourth verse: '*I sought the Lord, and he heard me, and delivered me from all my fears.*'" Just as he finished, Martha came to check on May. May told them she would like it if they would sing something.

As Joe and Josh were unhitching the horse, they heard singing coming from the house. Joe said, "This is so uplifting. I wish Sam could be here all the time."

Sunday morning they went to church, and Josh met more of his cousins. The minister gave a heartwarming sermon on kindred-ship in Christ, where love reigns. That afternoon Sam and Martha went for a walk up the trail behind Joe and May's house. On their return they sat down on the log and had an opportunity to talk. Sam told Martha, "I feel that someday I want to get married, if it is the Lord's will. We will be going home tomorrow. Would you consider starting a courtship? We could start by writing to each other."

Martha smiled at the man she had just started to get to know. "I think you are a good Christian man, so yes, we can write. But I need to think about courting. I would not lead you on and then drop you, I really like our church, and I don't think I could leave Joe and May."

Sam said, "That attitude is what makes me like you. It's like Christ in you, the hope of Glory." When they parted, they agreed they would be friends, and would write, then see what the Lord had in mind for them.

The next day they headed for home after a teary farewell. Josh was so happy to have the opportunity to meet so many of his friends and cousins. He was getting tired and would be glad to be home. They stopped once in a town and put the horse in a livery barn to be fed and rest. They rented a cabin with two beds, which let Josh have a better night. The double bed they had shared at Joe's, while comfortable, caused for a restless night.

While they both enjoyed the trip and the fellowship, the sight of the home place was comforting. Amos, seeing them arrive, came over to welcome them home. He told Josh he was sorry, but one of Josh's horses had died the night before. They went out to see it, and Josh said, "That horse was old, and I have been expecting him to go for a while now," he assured Amos. "It wasn't anything you did that caused it."

That was a relief to Amos, and he said, "Come over for supper, and then ma and I can hear about your trip." That sounded good to them, so they went.

When Mary heard of the plans, she asked Alice if she could bring a pot of chili soup over. Alice said, "Why yes, if you can come too?"

Mary said, "I'll see what John thinks, but I'm almost sure it will be fine with him."

The soup was delicious and they had an enjoyable conversation. Josh told them about all the old friends and cousins he got to see whom he hadn't seen for a long time. He said he wanted to tell about what Joe told him the day he and Joe were together. "Joe told me about the time they felt sure an angel sent Sam to their rescue. Joe had nothing but good to say about you Sam."

This made Sam blush, "It wasn't me, it was the Lord in my heart that did that. Dad, I had gone a long way from home and the things you taught me. After I was down and out, I opened the little Bible you gave me when I was a boy. It happened to open to the scripture where Jesus taught about the evil spirit going out of a man. How it comes back and finds him empty, he takes seven spirits worse than himself, and the last condition of that man is worse than the first. When I read that passage I shivered to think what might become of me. I wondered how I could fill my life with the holy things of God to keep the unclean spirit out. Dad, it was then I remembered the evenings when John and I were young. John would be on your lap and I on mothers, and you sang the good old songs of Zion."

"I still can see the oil lamp on the stand between you and mother. You would rock and sing until we almost went to sleep, then you would put us in bed. As I went into a deep sleep I would still hear you singing."

"Those songs instilled deep within me, are what filled my heart with the love of God, as I made my way back home. It was one of those songs Joe and May heard me singing behind their house that night a long time ago when she was sick and needed help. That's why they think an angel sent me to them."

John nodded, "Yes, I too remember those days, and I think it had an impact on my life."

Amos and Alice looked at each other and smiled as he said, "Pass it on boys."

Josh looked at the boys and said, "That was the most valuable education you have gotten."

The evening passed quickly with Sam and Josh sharing their experiences as well as hearing about the events at home while they were gone. Sam tickled little Susie under the chin and said she had changed a lot. He missed her.

Sam was soon busy with his construction jobs, and had to discipline himself, lest he not keep his heart full of the love of God. He couldn't get his mind off of Martha. He decided to write to her and tell her about their trip home.

Dear Martha,

Life here is going on as usual. Little Susie is sure growing. At church Sunday a lot of people, wanted to know about the folks over there at Jeffrey, West Virginia. I tried to explain the love shown there is as the love here. I am being busy as I want to be. I have to tell myself to not neglect the Word of God. I pray daily for Joe and May. They are such sincere devout Christians. When I think of them, I think of you. We have several good Christian girls here; but none which impress me as much as you. The sacrificing love you show toward Joe and May is very noticeable.

It has been three months since we left there, and I have been praying about our relationship. I feel led to ask for your hand in wedlock. Take all the time you want, and listen for the still small voice. We both want to be guided by the Lord. I know you don't want to leave Joe's and I don't want you to. I've been thinking we could live in the Jeffrey area. I'm sure there is a need for carpenters there too. We know there is a loving church. Take your time and pray about it. When your answer comes I'll be happy to hear.

May the Lord bless you,
Sam

The days passed and Sam didn't hear anything from Martha. Sometimes he was discouraged, and Satan tried to tell him to give up and go enjoy himself. He even had some of the worldly people he worked for try to get him to do things the church frowned on. The darkest time was when he was told that a rumor was going around he had cheated one of his customers. In reality it was the other way around. A customer had failed to pay what he agreed to, so Sam just took the loss. Now to have the customer tell some of the brethren Sam had cheated him. This was about more than Sam could take.

Then another rumor started circulating that Sam had been impure with Martha when they were there, and that she had repented but he hadn't. And that now he wanted to marry her, but she didn't want such a bad man. It was this rumor that gave Satan an advantage, and Sam was beginning to become bitter. At times he felt he no longer wanted to go to church. He soon was spending more time at work and neglected his devotions. When he did remember to read his Bible he could not concentrate on what he was reading. Satan was getting an upper hand.

It didn't take long before Josh saw something was wrong with Sam. He just wasn't the same as before. He was very sullen and cast down. Josh went over and talked to Amos about it. Alice said, "I have heard a little, but I don't believe it's true."

Mary noticed Josh on the front porch talking to her in-laws and joined the conversation. She told them what she had heard, "Someone wrote to Martha and passed some bad untruths to her."

Josh said, "I'll talk to Sam and write to Martha to get this straight."

That evening when Sam came home, Josh had the chores done. He asked Sam to come sit down a little. He brought up the rumor and asked Sam about it. Sam sat there and shook. He said, "There isn't any truth in it. Why would someone tell something like that? I have been trying hard to walk a Christian life and now this."

Josh said, "Satan is alive and well. You need to talk to your father. I'm going to write to Martha."

Sam wasted no time going over to his parents. After Sam told his dad all the things that had happened to him, Amos didn't seem to be excited about it. He said, "Son, let's pray first." After petitioning the Lord for wisdom Amos said, "Son there is not much you can do about it. Tell me, what did you do about the man that didn't pay you?"

"All I knew to do was to forgive the debt," Sam answered.

Amos said, "Now you can pray for him, which I believe you have already done."

Sam raised his eyebrows, "How did you know?"

Amos said, "Because his conscience is bothering him. So, to try to cover it up, he is telling that you cheated him. As for the other rumor, you and the Lord know the truth. Sam, you have been doing so good, both spiritually and materially, so don't be surprised that Satan is trying you."

Sam said, "But some of this gossip is coming from some of the church members, which ought not to be."

Amos said, "So true son, but think of our Lord Jesus. Who was it that condemned him to death? Was it not his people? Yet on the cross he cried out, 'Father forgive them, they know not what they do.' Also, Peter said of Jesus, '*when reviled, he reviled not again, when suffered, he threatened not, but committed himself to him who judges righteous.*' Son, remember the words of John when he came to the house? How he forgave you and has never had any ill feelings toward you? Now son, work hard to fill your heart with the good things of God, and try to forget the wrong done to you. Be sure to pray for those who despitefully used you. In the end, you'll be stronger."

Sam went home with a lot of things to think about. He was thankful for a dad with wisdom as he had. He told Josh what his father told him. Josh told Sam, "There was a deacon in the building business, who built a barn for a worldly man. He did a good job. When he turned in the bill, the man told him he was not going to pay the deacon. You claim to be non resistant, so I won't pay you, and I'll see if you go to the law to collect it. The deacon said in that case the only way to get it off the books is to forgive it. So that is what he done."

"Years later, as the man was getting older and approaching death, his conscious bothered him so much that he went to the deacon and apologized for what he had done. He wanted to pay the debt. The deacon told him there was no debt, as he had forgiven it a long time ago. The man was beside himself and said he had to get this off his mind before he died. The man asked, 'How can I rectify what I have done?' The deacon told him to give the amount to charity and pray the Lord would forgive him."

Sam said, "Thank you. Just knowing others have suffered like things seems to help."

Josh replied, "Be sure to keep your heart full of the love of God. Remember the scripture; '*They who will live godly in Christ Jesus will suffer persecution.*'" Josh told him he had written to Martha and felt all would be okay there. Two weeks later Sam got a letter from Martha.

> *Dear Sam,*
>
> *Greetings in the name of Jesus, I wanted to write and let you know I have been praying about your proposal. Joe and May are going downhill. They desire that you come for a visit. They would like for you to live with them. When you wrote you said maybe you would live over here. There is a need for builders here too. I've been thinking that we could move in with them. One night in my dream I heard a still small voice saying give a positive answer to your question. The answer to your proposal is yes.*
>
> *I talked it over with my parents, also with our minister. They all were told by Joe and May about the blessings they received by you when you were here. They felt to move in with them would be a sacrifice on our part, but I told them both you and I feel we are servants of our God. May we not tarry too long. Hope to hear from you soon.*

May the Lord guide you,
Martha.

Sam was so overjoyed, that he went over to his folks and shared with them the response to his proposal. Amos and Alice were happy to hear the news and said it was commendable of them to move in with Joe's. It would be a sacrifice on their part, but if they, from their heart, wanted to do that, then they would be blessed. Sam said, "We feel it to be a privilege to be an instrument in the hands of the Lord."

Amos said, "Son, we will miss you, but knowing you are getting a Christian wife, and you will be a workman in the vineyard of the Lord, we wish you the best."

When Sam told Josh about their plans, he had a smile on his face. He was afraid Josh would be disappointed he was leaving, but he didn't seem to mind at all. Josh asked, "Do you know when you will be leaving?"

Sam answered, "As soon as I get the barn done I'm working on, which will be in about three weeks."

Josh said, "That will work out fine. I hadn't told anyone, but I am getting married to Margaret Sleaybal in two weeks. We talked about you, and she didn't want to make you move out. Especially so soon after the valley you have been through. Sam, she believes in you and thinks you've done marvelously in forgiving the wrong done to you. The timing will work out just right, as we can stay in her house a few days."

Josh added, *"All things work together for good to them who love the Lord."*

The Wedding
Chapter 12

Sam finished the barn as quickly as he could. He wrote to Martha and said he would come as soon as he could get things in order. Josh offered to let him use a team of his horses and the spring wagon to move his belongings.

Two weeks later Josh and Margaret were married in a private wedding, with only the preacher and his wife attending. They felt being a second marriage for both of them, it would be better to keep it small. Josh temporarily moved in with Margaret until Sam was ready to move.

Sam got a letter one day from Martha. She wrote that Joe and May offered him the spare bedroom. She would come and help when needed, but with the help of her younger sister, June.

A month after Sam received Martha's acceptance letter, he was ready to head toward West Virginia. The trip with the loaded spring wagon took him almost a week to get there. Often Sam thought about how not too many years ago, he was headed the other way with only a backpack and an old sleeping bag. The fact that God had blessed him was a truth he never wanted to forget.

It was getting toward evening when he arrived. Joe heard him coming and met him in the driveway. He said, "You may put the team and the spring wagon in the shed behind the house."

After Sam backed the wagon into the shed, he unhitched the team and led them to water at the tank by the spring. He put the team in the stable, unharnessed them, and gave them a little grain he had brought along. He was out of hay, but Joe had some and said he was welcome to it.

He carried his suitcase in and was welcomed by May. Although she was frail, she had the same smile on her face. She was so delighted to know about him and Martha's plans to wed, and more delighted to think they would consider living with them. It seemed as if that knowledge just buoyed her up.

Sam went over to talk to Martha and her parents about the wedding. By mutual agreement they decided on the fifteenth of November. There was a lot of getting ready to do. Decisions needed to be made: as whom to invite, who to marry them, and what they would serve. Martha wanted to keep it plain and simple. She suggested they have it in the Meeting House after church with those at the meeting to be the guests. She thought if it would be alright with Sam, they have Jacob, her minister, to marry them and have his Uncle Ronald preach the sermon. That plan sounded good to him, so they approached Jacob about it. He said that would be an acceptable plan.

They sent a letter to Uncle Ronald, and soon got a response. Uncle Ronald wrote they would be glad to come and he would try to meet their request. A letter arrived from his folks saying they and John's planned to come. Josh wrote they would like to come, but they had some sickness and may not feel well enough, but wished them God's blessings.

Sam's parents and John's arrived two days before the wedding. Then Uncle Ronald's came the next afternoon. Joe and May wanted Amos' to stay at their home, and asked Sam if there were any way he could arrange it. Sam said his parents could have his room and Mary could sleep on the couch. He and John could sleep on floor beds. They could fix a place for Susie by the couch.

Uncle Ronald's stayed at Jacob's home. Plenty of the Church members offered places for the cousins.

The wedding day dawned with clear skies and a pleasant breeze out of the south. Sam was so nervous as he went over to Martha's home. Together they walked with her parents to the meeting house. Soon after they got there, in pulled Josh and Margaret. That brought a smile to Sam's face.

They were expected to sit on the front bench with their parents. Amos noticed the meeting house was almost filled to capacity and thought, "Sam and Martha are surely liked here."

Jacob opened the service with a hymn and some encouraging remarks. After which they kneeled in prayer as he poured out his thankfulness to our God and asked for His blessings on the day.

Uncle Ronald asked for the reading of Saint Matthew nineteen. Amos, being a deacon, read it. They then sang another song, and Uncle Ronald gave a very inspiring sermon on the home and what makes a godly home. It was very encouraging. He then had a closing prayer.

Jacob stood up and announced, "There is a couple getting married today, and all are invited to stay." Then he asked Sam and Martha to stand up. He went over some of the things Ronald talked about such as love, faithfulness, forgiveness, and responsibility. Jacob then asked the couple to join right hands, and he asked Sam, *"Do you Sam Wagoner take Martha, whose hand you now hold, to be your lawful wedded wife? Do you promise to love, honor and cherish her, in joy or sorrow, in health or sickness, in prosperity or adversity, and forsaking all others cleave only to her as long as you both shall live?"*

Sam said, "I do."

Then Jacob turned to Martha and said, *"Do you Martha Jones take Sam, whose hand you now hold to be your lawful wedded husband? Do you promise to love, honor and cherish him, in joy and sorrow, in health and sickness, in prosperity or adversity, and forsaking all others cleave only to him as long as you both shall live?"*

Martha said, "I do."

Jacob continued, "By the authority invested in me by the Church and according to the laws of the state of West Virginia, I pronounce you husband and wife. What God has joined together let not man put asunder."

The couple kissed and then knelt in prayer as tears slipped down Alice's face. Jacob then introduced the newlyweds as, "Mr. and Mrs. Sam Wagoner." The congregation sang, *Blest be the tie that binds our hearts in Christian love.*

They were dismissed, and a lot of people stayed around to congratulate them. It was announced that the members had brought together food for a meal in the conservation building. All were invited to come and enjoy this couple's first dinner together as husband and wife.

Sam and Martha enjoyed the meal together with their families and others they knew. Martha met some of Sam's cousins and friends, and Sam met some of hers. Joe and May were at the wedding, but didn't feel well enough to stay for the dinner, so June took them home. One of the church sisters went along and told her she would get their dinner and stay with them so June could be with her family.

After everyone was finished eating, a table was set up and some of the younger girls brought the wedding gifts for the couple to open. One at a time they opened the gifts and thanked the giver. Most were useful items, which would be helpful in the future. The last item was only a little envelope, which when Sam slit open and handed to Martha, she pulled out a slip of paper and together they read,

> *Dear Sam and Martha,*
>
> *We didn't bring anything as we just decided at the last minute we could come. We would like for you to accept the team and spring wagon we loaned to you for your move as a gift from us. We wish you two a happy and blessed married life.*
>
> *May the Lord bless,*
> *Josh and Margaret*

Sam looked at Josh and had trouble holding back the tears as he emotionally said, "Thank you."

A parting hymn was sung, and then Ronald offered a prayer for the couple and those who would be traveling home. He thanked the Lord for such a beautiful day, as it was the beginning of a new day in several lives.

Amos' and John's were to stay at Martha's parents' as Sam and Martha wanted to spend their first night at Joe and May's. Holding hands, they waved to the people, as they started walking towards Joe's. When they got close, they went up to the trail and walked to the log behind their house. Hand in hand they stood there and sang, *Rock of ages shelter me, let me hide myself in thee.* As they finished, there was Joe with his cane. He said, "Come on down, May is expecting you."

When they got to the house, May had a smile on her face as she said, "Now you are home."

That evening was special to Sam's as Joe and May told of their wedding and the early years of their married life. They told of the good things and the sorrowful times. They told of the changes they have seen and the disappointments along the way. When they got married they wanted to have a large family, but found it was not to be. They said they were thankful to have one son, but they had no grandchildren. They told of the many blessings they had received, and of a time they were mistreated with slander and rebuked. But the Lord was with them, and they were made stronger by the persecution. They said it was hard to forgive, but with God's help they overcame it and from their hearts forgave. They shared with them many more stories of their lives which were very interesting. They said, "The best day was when we heard someone singing on the hill behind our house. We feel it was surely an angel that sent you. Now, Sam we think of you and Martha as our son and daughter, sent to us by our God." After the evening devotion and prayer they retired for the night.

New Responsibilities
Chapter 13

The first few weeks were a time of adjusting for all of them. May had trouble giving up her kitchen, but was glad to have help. Martha kept the place clean, and as May was getting weaker, she knew it was needed. Martha was kind and patient, careful not to go ahead too quickly. Joe was encouraging to both of them. He talked to May about the blessing of having Sam's there to take care of things.

May said, "Yes I know, but it is hard not being able to do our work. I know this is the way God ordained things to be, and we are so thankful for Sam and Martha. Please tell me when I'm getting out of place."

Once in a while Joe would say to her, "Remember?" Then May would smile and say, "Oh! Yes!" then look at Martha and say, "I'm sorry." Martha would look at her and smile.

Sam and Joe walked around the place, and Joe pointed to things that needed repaired and said, "I'm just not able to maintain things as I should any more."

Sam said, "I'll try to get them taken care of as I can. Now I need to find some work."

It wasn't long until work started coming in. The first was for a neighbor who wanted a barn built. It wasn't a large building, but it gave him a start. By the time it was complete, there was a man from town who needed a garage built onto his house. In the evenings Sam found time to do some of the much-needed repairs at home.

He limited his time on the job as he felt home came ahead of work. He was always able to help Martha when she needed him. There were times they would go into their bedroom and talk together about things. They made sure they always had time for their devotions. Joe and May gently helped the young couple keep their priorities right.

The church members were amazed that a newly married couple would move in with an older couple and take care of them. They felt it was commendable, and they offered to relieve them at times.

Sam told Martha it was nice of them to offer to help and they should accept their offer at times. He suggested that about every two weeks she let someone take her place and she go spend the day with her folks. That was a help to Martha. There were times they both went over and Sam would help Daniel with a project he was doing. Sam and Daniel became close, which made Martha happy. Sam always enjoyed going to her folks. They had so many things in common.

Martha made sure Joe and May always got their medicine on time and the right amount. Both Joe and May seemed to improve in health probably as a result of proper diet and the right medicine.

Three years rolled by and Sam's were expecting to have their first baby. Daniel and Amanda were concerned about the arrangement with Joe's. They were getting feebler and needed more care. Joe said they wanted to give their home to Sam and Martha. Sam was not comfortable with that but told Joe, "How would it be if we bought it from you?"

Joe said, "Our son will be coming next week and we'll talk about it."

The next Tuesday their son Steven came. He had been there several times since Sam and Martha had moved in. He was so impressed at how good his folks were doing in their care.

When Joe told Steven that Sam wanted to buy the place, Steven said, "With all they have done for you why sell it? Just give it to them."

Sam spoke up and said, "We are not helping them for that purpose; we feel it is our calling."

Steven said, "What you have done is more valuable than the price of the property."

Joe said, "Son, what about your inheritance?"

Steven said, "What these folks have done for you is more comforting to me than all the money in the world. And besides I have more than I need, so give it to them."

When Sam saw that they were determined to give them the place he said, "If that is what you want, then we'll humbly accept it. I have been thinking it would be nice if I would build a room across the end of the house and put in a bathroom to make it easier for Joe and May. The added space would give Joe's a peaceful place to take their naps. If you give us this place, I'll build that room and it will be theirs as long as they need it."

May said, "Sam your angel is still leading you." Tears welled up in his eyes.

A few weeks later the legal work was completed, and Sam's became the owners of the estate. Daniel and Amanda were excited about the deal. Daniel wanted to help on the addition. When the church members heard about it, there were several wanting to help. Sam put in the footing and on a set day they had a raising, which brought in a lot of folks. A plumber from town heard about what they were doing and offered to put in the bath plumbing for a small fee. One of the members told the plumber, "When you do the job, give me the bill."

From the day Sam started to lay the foundation until the addition was completed was just five weeks. Joe and May were overwhelmed. Steven came and helped move their things into the new room. Joe said, "It just doesn't seem right to not go out to the little building by the garden."

Two years rolled by, and James Edward was added to the family. By now little Amos Joe was walking all around. They had trouble with him wanting to go into Joe's room. Martha pulled the door part way shut, but May protested saying she wanted to see him. She called him her little angel. Joe and May were delighted to have two little grandsons come into their lives, even though they spent a lot of time in bed.

Sam had a long list of customers waiting for their projects to be built, but he made sure to take an appropriate amount of time to help others in need and also at home. The church sisters came in almost daily to help care for Joe and May. Many times they would help Martha, and always wanted to play with little Amos. They felt to do so was a blessing.

Sam's folks came occasionally, and even more now that they had a little grandson named after Amos. John's came too. Susie was a big girl, and she had a little sister, Joy, and twin brothers, Ray and Roy. There were several in the family. They were always a joy when they came. Good bye was always hard.

A council meeting was held one Saturday morning, and Jacob told the congregation he felt he needed some help in the ministry. He took the voice, asking if the members would be willing to give him help. The voice was willing to do so. There was a fervent prayer the Lord would place who he would in the position of minister. It was a very solemn meeting. Likely everyone there was praying the Holy Spirit would lead.

When the Elders came out, it was so quiet you could hear a pin drop. Then one of them said, "Sam and Martha Wagoner have been chosen to the ministry." Tears began to flow. The members all received them into this office with many tears and much encouragement. For them, it was the beginning of another new day.

In the evening devotions, Joe in his feeble, quivering voice, prayed a very tender plea to the Lord to empower Sam by the Holy Spirit that he be a good minister of the word of God. Sam felt an old father in the faith had just poured out his heart to God in his behalf. Tears ran down his face, and he heard May and Martha sobbing.

Sam didn't sleep well that night. Many thoughts were on his mind. He thought, "If John were to be a preacher he would likely be a much better one, as he was the book worm when we were young."

Jacob and Merial came over and gave them much encouragement. Jacob said, "Remember what God told Moses when he said he didn't speak well? God asked Moses, 'Who made man's mouth?'" Jacob said, "Be yourself, Sam. Don't try to be someone you're not. Satan will try to discourage you, and if he fails with that, he'll try to make you think more of yourself than you ought."

Sam's mind went to the little book, and what he had read about filling our heart with good things of God so Satan can't get in. He thought, "It sure is a blessing we have the little book, the Word of God." Jacob had many other things to tell him, which he much appreciated.

Later that week Sam got an encouraging letter from his father. He wrote to never doubt the power of God. "Always put your trust in the leading of the Holy Spirit. After you have preached a sermon, thank the Lord for leading you. It is his work, and you are his servant." Then he quoted the psalm, *Except the Lord build the house, they labor in vain who build it.*

Sam tried to keep his mind on his work as he had a lot to do. There were several customers waiting their turn to have their project done. He wondered how he was going to satisfy them and preach too. Then he remembered Jacob told him to enter into it slowly as the Lord provides. He decided to not work on the job more than six hours a day. He remembered the falling of trees and after he backed off to six hours a day they seemed to get more done than when they worked from dawn to dark. Each evening after devotions, when Joe and May had gone into their room, they would put the boys to bed and study a little. Someone told him a little, little, little, makes a lot. After the Saturday work was done he found time to study some. The question was what to study. He decided to ask Jacob.

They were nervous as they walked to the meeting house Sunday morning. He didn't know if Jacob would ask him to do anything or not. Jacob called an ingathering hymn. Then he read from the twenty third Psalm. He then looked at Sam and said he could call a hymn to be sung and open meeting and have prayer. Sam felt a chill run down his back, and then he remembered the dream a long time ago. It was about an angel who would be with him as he went towards home. He thought, "Yes, I'm still heading toward home, our Father's home." He named a song in the little book, number sixty nine.

Father, I stretch my hands to thee,
No other help I know
If thou withdraw thyself from me
Ah, whether can I go?

What did thine only son endure?
Before I took my breath
 What pain what labor to secure
My Soul from second death.

Author of faith to thee I lift,
My weary longing eyes,
Oh may I now receive that gift
My Soul without it dies.

After they were finished singing there wasn't a dry eye in the building. Sam opened his Bible to the now familiar scripture about the empty person and how the unclean spirit will take seven more spirits worse than himself and the last of that man is worse than the first. He said, "We come together today to have our hearts filled with the holy things of God. That will not happen if we sleep. We must open our hearts to receive the word spoken. If we work too late on Saturday night, we will not get the rest this earthly body needs. Then we come to church on Sunday morning and try to understand what we are hearing. A tired individual, when not in motion will fall to sleep. It's the way God made us. It's the way the body regenerates. What I'm trying to say is, we need to get our rest before coming here to the house of the Lord. To come here and sleep, we miss out on a wonderful opportunity to strengthen our inner man. Let us pray."

Jacob opened his Bible to the fourteenth chapter of Saint John, and read the first few verses, and then preached about blessings we have of the home over on the other shore. He seemed so enthused; it made the congregation feel they were ready to go anytime. He said our lives should be lived so we would be ready to go at a moment's notice. He made mention of the Israelites leaving Egypt at midnight, and not knowing when the time would come, but to be ready. He said, "Are you ready?"

On the way home, Sam told Martha he felt the Spirit was sure working with Jacob today. He had so many inspiring things to say. Martha said, "Yes, it was working with both of our ministers today."

Sam took a hold of her hand and gave it a squeeze, and brushing a tear from his eye said, "Thank you. We truly need the Holy Spirit of God to help us."

Martha said, "Yes, and all of us need the Lord's help."

The Ministry
Chapter 14

Sam continued to study a little each day and kept his work on schedule. He really liked the construction work, yet he wanted to make the Lord's work his priority. It seemed Sundays came so soon. Jacob didn't push him, but gave him all the opportunity he wanted. Every time after he preached he felt so built up in the Spirit. He asked Jacob what to talk about. Jacob said, "Sam, you need to pray and fast, and then the Lord will bring something. As you continue to study the Bible, you will find it full of things to speak about."

Two years went by and the load didn't seem much lighter. He had taken the text four times. Jacob stopped by one day and talked to Sam about visiting the church over in Logan County, "We should go help them at their Love Feast."

Sam shivered to think about doing that. "Let us think about it over night. We will let you know in the morning."

That evening Sam talked to Joe and May about the weekend. Joe said he thought they ought to go and trust in the Lord to help him. May said, "I feel you are doing well with the ministry and would be a help to the dear members over there. They have been having some struggles. With your past experiences you could be an encouragement to them."

While they were still talking, Martha's folks showed up for a visit and got in on the conversation. Amanda volunteered to stay with Joe's while they were gone. Daniel said, "Son that will be a good work to go and help them. They will be delighted to have both of you at their meeting."

Martha turned to May and said, "Do you think you will be okay while we are gone?"

May smiled and said, "Oh yes, we just wish we could go too."

The next day Sam told Jacob their decision, so it was decided when they would leave. Sam had to work harder on the job to have time to leave, yet still thought he needed to study in order to make the trip. Martha told him to just slow down and trust the Lord to guide.

The day came for them to go and Sam told Martha he didn't feel very good as he had a stomach ache. May said to Martha, "Fix him some tea. That will likely help him." The trip took three hours and as they traveled Jacob had some good things to tell him. He was such a spirit minded man and knew so many scriptures with the meaning of them. He told Sam to stay away from controversial subjects while he was trying to learn. "There is a need of sound preaching which can be gotten from the old stories in the Bible, and they are easy to learn." That was encouraging to Sam. By the time they arrived, he had forgotten all about his tummy ache.

They went to Josiah and Alma Brubakers to spend the night. Josiah was the elder of the church district. They received a hearty welcome. Josiah sent the travelers to the house while he unhitched the horse, fed and watered him. Alma showed them in and to their rooms. Then she said, "Come on into the living room and rest yourselves a bit." When they walked into the room, they were surprised to see Uncle Ronald's and Sam's folks there. There were hugs and kisses, and Amos and Alice picked up their grandsons and gave them loving hugs.

That was a joy in two ways. To get to be with them, and, as Ronald was a preacher, it would take some of the work off Sam. He was all smiles.

Alma made a good supper, and they had such a good visit. Sam felt he was in school to be in the company of two seasoned preachers and a deacon. Their talk was almost all about the Christian walk of life, so up-building and more also being just before their communion. After spending the evening listening to them, Sam felt more fortified to enter the work of the Love Feast.

They had a good night's sleep. The morning dawned bright and clear. The birds were singing, and Sam asked Martha, "Doesn't the sound of the birds make us want to go to the house of prayer, doubting nothing?"

She smiled and said, "And with no stomach ache."

Alma had a small breakfast fixed and some orange juice. Ministers usually don't like to eat much before a meeting.

When the meeting started they sang an inviting song. Ronald opened with words of encouragement and led them to prayer. Jacob gave a powerful message leading up to the communion. Sam closed with song and prayer. There was some service in the afternoon. The communion started at five that evening. Jacob had the main part, and Ronald and Sam helped. The preaching by all three of them, along with the singing, was so inspiring and uplifting. Having communed with each other and the Lord, they felt they were close to Heaven.

They spent the night with Josiah's, and the next morning they went back to the meeting house for a farewell service. Sam was told it would be his responsibility to begin the service. There would be no prayer at the beginning, but one at the closing. They were to divide the time.

Meeting time came, and the house was filled to capacity. Sam sat there wondering what to start out on. Then he remembered what Jacob told him, about the stories in the Bible and how they will lead us to Christ. He remembered the condensed account of Joseph, which his father read to him and his brother when they were young. The chills ran down his back. Then his mind rolled to the angel that led him on his way home. He thought, "We are all on our way homeward," so he named the hymn five twenty-two: *I'm a lonely traveler here.*

As the last line of the last verse died out he opened his Bible to Genesis forty-five, and read verse three: "*Then Joseph said to his brothers, 'I am Joseph; does my father still live?' But his brothers could not answer him, for they were dismayed in his presence."* Sam said, "I am Joseph! How do you think those ten brothers felt when they heard these words? Here was the man who they feared and the one who had all authority in Egypt. He had the power to put them in prison, or to make slaves of them, or to destroy them if he wanted to. Their very lives were in the hollow of his hand. Did he exercise that authority? Yes he did, but in a much different way than a lot of men would have. For one thing, he had always obeyed God and put his trust in him. Another, he never became bitter. Another, he didn't allow hatred into his heart."

Using these thoughts, Sam preached a tear jerking sermon and summed it up with thoughts on forgiveness and love.

Ronald continued on with more of the same thoughts. Then Jacob finished up, putting the cap sheaf on it all. They kneeled as Jacob opened his heart to the Lord in fervent praise and thanksgiving with tears of farewell prayer.

A lunch was served, and then it was time to bid farewell. There were a lot of tears shed as they bade Uncle Ronald's and Sam's folk's good bye. Alice had to hug young Amos Joe and James.

The trip homeward was somewhat solemn as they were tired and felt they had left a loving people behind. They were glad for the spiritual build up of the meeting.

As usual, it was good to see home. Daniel and Amanda were glad to see them and had a lot of questions about the meeting. Amanda said, "Joe and May had their medication and went to sleep soon after devotions."

The next day, Joe awoke with a head ache. May soon awoke and wanted to know about the meeting. They said those meetings are so uplifting. They remembered having gone to the one they were to, but it was years ago. They talked to the boys a little, but it was evident they didn't feel well.

They ate a little breakfast, and then went to sleep. Martha told Sam, "Grandpa's aren't acting right."

Sam said, "I noticed that too, I think I'll not go to work for awhile."

The elderly couple awoke at noon but weren't like they usually were. Martha heard them talking, and then she heard May call for her. When she went into their room, Joe said they wanted to be anointed this evening. He said, "Steven is coming at five, so could it be then?" Martha went to the door and called Sam to come in. Sam said he would get in touch with Jacob right away.

Jacob was glad to come, and said, as they always enjoyed singing so well, he thought they should contact some other of the Church members to come and sing afterward. They mentioned it to Joe and May who said, "That would be nice, and Steven would like that too."

May added, "I sure hope we can stay awake that long."

A little before five, Steven came and soon Jacob's arrived. Sam told Steven about his folk's request. He was happy they asked for that, as it is a good thing to do. He said, "I was here while you were gone, and noticed the folks were going downhill fast."

Joe and May were able to answer the questions clearly and were in submissive mind to whatever the Lord's will was. Joe's voice was quivery, and May was so weak they could hardly hear her. Jacob put the oil on Joe's head, then he and Sam laid their hands on Joe and prayed for healing, forgiveness of any sins, and for a comforting of his conscience, the Lord's will be done. Then they anointed May. They also laid their hands on her and prayed as they did for Joe. There were a lot of tears running down cheeks.

After a short period of quiet meditation, they began to sing. Joe asked for *Nearer my God to Thee.* The house was nearly full, and the singing was beautiful.

When they were finished with that song, Joe said, "I'm ready to be with the Lord."

May was having trouble staying awake during the song, although there were tears coming from her eyes. Feebly, she asked to sing *Rock of Ages*. She said, "That song was so comforting to me the first time we seen Sam and it will be now too."

As they started singing, Joe put his hand in May's. When they sang the last line, and as the last note faded away, May took her last breath. Joe said, "My May, she is gone." He started sobbing uncontrollably.

Sam wasn't ready for this although he knew it was coming. He sat on the bed by Joe and they sobbed together. Steven sat by Sam and the three were in deep grief. Everyone was crying. After a little time Jacob offered a comforting prayer. Joe kept holding onto May's hand saying, "My May, my May."

The man from the mortuary came and took May's body. When Joe watched them taking her away, he fainted. His breathing came in gasps, and nothing they could do helped. Jacob and Merial, along with Sam and Martha, took him to the hospital. Ladies from the church put the house in order and closed it up.

At the hospital Joe was revived, but very feebly. He didn't say anything about May. The second day he asked, "Where is May?" and then drifted asleep again. Some from the church stayed with Joe and Steven all the time.

Josiah Brubaker came and helped Jacob with May's funeral. It was a tender time for Sam. He thought of the closeness of her and Joe and their concerns for each other. Jacob pointed out the blessed hope we have after life here is finished. Josiah said, "This is the completion of a good fight, now for the crown." Sam and Martha knew this is what May was living for and she was at a better home. Ties of loved ones are hard to break.

After the funeral Sam and Martha went back to the hospital. Joe would come and go and at times ask for May. After two days, the doctor told them to go home and get some rest.

The Horseless Carriage
Chapter 15

It was a nice, spring day. The birds were singing so beautifully, and the pleasant air was balmy after the shower. It was one of those days a person felt thankful to be alive. As Sam walked from the mailbox toward the house he wondered what might be in the envelope they got that day from Josh.

As he opened the door he was greeted with a cheerful, although feeble, good morning. Joe was in his wheel chair looking out the window. It was apparent he was feeling much better than he had for some time. In his hand was his coffee cup, and a smile was on his face.

Sam had gotten a call early from Jacob asking him to help with anointing an older sister of the church. She was feeling very sick, and knowing she had cancer, thought this might be the day of her death. She lived with her daughter and son-in-law about two miles away. Sam never turned down anyone who needed him, day or night.

Martha had a breakfast of fried hominy and sausage gravy. She asked Sam to bring Joe to the table, as it was ready. The children were still asleep. As Sam pushed him up to the table he said, "I picked up the mail on the way in, and there is a letter from Josh." After they gave thanks for their food, Martha asked about Sister Ruth. Sam said, "It seemed to be such a comfort to her to be anointed. It is a special closeness to the Lord on such occasions."

Joe remarked about the time he and May were anointed, how comforting it was. He said, "Little did we know how close we were to our reward. May was ready to go, and I thought I was too, but the Lord saw it different. I could sense her departure, and then woke up in the hospital."

Martha said, "Yes, and that was three weeks later."

Joe said, "We certainly are in the hands of a just God who does all things well. I'm glad Sister Ruth got comfort."

As they ate their breakfast, Sam slit open the envelope, being curious as to what Josh had to say.

Dear Sam and Martha,

Greetings in Jesus' name. We were glad to get the letter Martha wrote to us explaining Joe's condition. It is marvelous how the Lord works in our lives when we live for him. Joe and May were a living example of trusting in the Lord and never complaining. The suffering Joe went through in the hospital, and never complaining as he gradually regained his strength is wonderful. We are so glad that after six weeks in the hospital, he was able to come home. Steven told us of the faithfulness of the two of you in being there for him all those days. Surely the Lord will bless you for all the kindness.

If the Lord will, we plan to come next week. I hope Joe is able to visit some as we feel blessed with his advice and counsel.

With love,
Josh and Margaret

Amos Joe came out about this time and said, "Is Grandpa Josh coming to see us?"

Sam said, "Yes son, it sounds like they will."

Amos Joe asked, "Is Grandpa and Grandma Wagoner coming too?"

Martha said, "No son, they didn't say anything about your grandparents coming."

James woke up. Martha got him out of his crib and came back to the table. Sam picked up Amos as he opened the Bible and read to them the fifteenth chapter of Saint John about the vine.

When he was finished Joe said, "It is so important to keep attached to the vine. Then, when you grow old as I am, the thought of passing on only looks brighter."

Tuesday, just before noon, there was a noise coming down the road, and here came an automobile. It slowed down and turned into their drive. It was a model A Ford, four door car, and Josh was the driver. On the other side, in the front, was Amos Wagoner. In the back seat sat Alice and Margaret. Sam and Martha were delighted to see them, and after hugs and kisses, they went into the house. Amos Joe was really happy to see his Grandpas and Grandmas.

Joe was taking a nap when they arrived, but soon got up and was wheeled in his chair out to the living room. He was happy to see them, and especially Josh. It had been several years since they spent the day going to see Josh's cousins. They had a lot of things to talk about. Martha opened some chicken and noodles, and soon they had a good dinner.

Joe spotted the Ford and asked who owned that. Josh said it was his. A frown crossed Joe's brow. He asked, "What does the Church say about that?"

As Amos was a deacon, he spoke up and said, "The Church has always been careful to not take on things that are highly esteemed in the eyes of the world, as it is an abomination in the sight of God. We didn't use the automobile for many years, as it was a luxury both cost wise and popular demand."

"When Henry Ford started making them on the assembly line they became more affordable, so common people could afford them. Now it seems most everyone has one. It is not a prestige anymore to own a car. We considered it at council meeting, and came to the conclusion that, if the automobile is used in a practical way, the Lord will not be offended. This decision came through much prayer and fasting, with much discussion. We trust the Holy Spirit has led us in this." Joe didn't say much as it was something strange to him.

They had a nice visit, but Joe wanted to go to bed early, as he didn't get much of an afternoon nap. He had so much enjoyed his visit with friends. The rest visited awhile after Joe retired. At bed time Josh's went over to Daniel and Amanda's for the night.

The next day Josh came over and Joe said, "I would really like to go someplace in that horseless carriage." They helped him into the front seat, and Amos and Sam rode in back.

Little Amos said, "Go with grandpa?" Amos held his grandson on his lap as they went to see one of Josh's friends.

Joe was amazed that there was no horse to pull this buggy. He said, "Well the reaper was new one time, and now we use it. I guess the buggy was new since Jesus was here, and we use it. But we must be careful how we accept new things."

Amos said, "That is good advice. That is why we decide those things by the Church body and not individually."

Joe enjoyed the little ride and the visit with the family they went to see. They were surprised to see him come and were glad he was doing so well. His mind was keen, but his body was weak. After a little visit Josh thought it best that they get home, so to not tire Joe too much. They bid their host adieu, got into the horseless carriage and took Joe home. Joe couldn't stop talking about the buggy without a horse. When they got back, he was slow getting into the house and wanted to lay down for a bit.

The guests stayed until after Sunday, and were able to attend meeting with them. Josh went over to Sam's and took Joe to church in his car. He was so delighted to be able to attend meeting, even though he sat in his wheel chair.

It was Sam's responsibility to open the Word of God to the people that day. He talked about *Patient endurance.* Joe took in every word and sat there nodding his head in agreement. When they sang he tried to help but could only hum along.

After meeting was over, several folks wanted to speak to him and some did, but Sam cut their time short as Joe needed to get home. Josh took him home and helped to put him to bed for a rest.

On Monday morning, after a teary good bye, the two couples left for home. Josh said they could make it in one day now with the Ford along with the better roads. That is, if they didn't have too many flat tires.

As they stood there watching the sputtering car head down the gravel road Sam asked Martha, "Do you think the Church folks here will ever have the automobile?"

She responded, "The advice of your father was good, as we don't want to cause a rift in our little congregation. However, if we had a car we could visit the members that live farther away more often. A small truck would be a help with your carpentry work too."

Sam said, "Let's just have patience; maybe the Lord will open that door."

Sam became busier with the work, which was a challenge for him as he felt to spend time with his family and Joe. Many evenings, when he came home Martha would inform him there was company coming to see Joe, and she invited them to stay for supper. Sam always enjoyed that, as he got to hear their conversations with Joe. Joe's mind was keen, and he enjoyed sharing with others some of his life experiences. Most of what he talked about was the love of God and his plan for man. He liked to tell about times gone by in the Old Testament. How many faithful had to endure great conflicts when standing for what God commanded?

One of the visits was two families who came and brought supper. In the course of the evening one of them brought up the question, "How can we know if we may use some of the modern inventions, yet not offend our Lord?"

Joe responded, "The Church has authority to decide things that are not in the Bible. According to Matthew 16:16 after Peter said *Thou art the Christ, the Son of the living God.*

Those who make this confession and are baptized are those who are Christ's Church, and in verse nineteen Christ continued. *And I will give thee the keys of the kingdom of heaven: and whatsoever thou shalt bind on earth shall be bound in heaven: and whatsoever thou shalt loose on earth shall be loosed in Heaven."* He said, "Our Lord, when he was here, knew all these things that were to come, so on those who confessed him as the Son of God; he built His Church, and gave them the authority to make decisions. Of course, they weren't to change what he said."

Joe said, "Now, as for the automobile which the Church in Virginia agreed upon, it depends on how it is used if it offends our Lord. They said they were common there, so they weren't highly esteemed in the world anymore. That is happening here too, so maybe we could talk it over with the Church sometime to see if we could use it."

Sam talked to Jacob about what he was hearing from some of the members about the auto. Jacob said, "I have heard some talking about it too. I think it's time to present it to the congregation to see what they think."

Three weeks later there was a council meeting and the subject was presented. After much discussion and prayer, it was decided they could have the automobile, but were admonished to be careful how they were used. There were some who thought it would be better not to, but said they would submit to the majority. After that council it was several months before anyone purchased one, but by and by they started taking the place of horse and buggies in the church parking lot. Some of those would come and get Joe to take him to the doctor or other places he wanted to go. He would warn them about letting this horseless carriage become an idol. He did appreciate getting to go to church when he felt well enough, also to go visit some of the old members his age.

It was two years later when Sam's received word from Josh's that they and Amos' were coming. That was a pleasant message. When they arrived there were two cars, Josh and Margaret in one and Sam's folks in the other.

After their greetings, Josh wanted to take Sam for a ride. Josh said, "You drive!" Sam thought of the day when his father gave him the reins and had said, "You drive." It had been a long time since he had driven a car. He was a little nervous at first, but soon got on to it.

When they got home, Josh said, "Sam, this is your car. You can preach, and this is a little something I can do to help you with the responsibility to exalt the name of God. I'm getting too old to drive, so we talked it over and this is what we want to do.

Sam shed some tears and said, "Thank you. You have truly been a father to me."

The Lord's Way
Chapter 16

Sam had trouble using the automobile when he remembered the one he had years ago, how he had used it going to the world and the pleasures therein. He talked to Joe about it, and Joe gave him good counsel about using it for the Lord's work. He said, "You can visit those farther away than you used to, and also go to more meetings to preach the Word of God."

Joe seemed to be such an inspiration to him and the way he patiently endured his pain, never complaining. He enjoyed going to meetings, hearing the preaching and worshipping with the people of God.

Sam used the car to go to his work, which made it easier to get home earlier. That gave him more time with his family. Martha said, "Josh has been good to us. First giving us the team and wagon, now their car."

Sam said, "He is wise in so many ways. He knew we had agreed as a church to use them, or he would not give it to us. He also knew, if I had made well enough in the building business and had bought a new one, Satan would tempt me to think it was I who worked hard and had gotten this machine. Therefore, I could use it as I pleased."

Martha responded, "Brethren in Christ can help each other in more ways than monetary."

Sam said, "True, the first car I bought was mine, bought with my money for my pleasure and it went to the world. This car I didn't buy nor deserve, yet it was a gift to be used for the work of the Lord in His vineyard."

Martha added, "We are his servants. May we ever keep this in our hearts."

Sam took Jacob with him to Church Councils in other districts when called to come. These trips were so much easier now than they were in the horse and carriage, and let them get home earlier. Jacob remarked about it on the way home one time. He said, "I am getting old and will not see things you will in the way of world progress. Be on your guard against the allurements of worldly inventions, as Satan will likely use them to draw the Christians away from the simplicity of the truth."

They just got home from a trip to communion service at an adjoining district and as he pulled into the drive, Amos Joe and James came out saying "Daddy, daddy!" They ran up to him for a hug. Then Amos said, "Grandpa is sick, Mommy needs you, come quick." They entered the house to find Martha standing over Joe with a fan in her hand fanning him. Joe was sitting in his wheelchair slumped over in a sweat. Sam went to him and asked him if he hurt.

Joe just looked up at him and asked, "Was the meeting spirit inspired?"

Sam responded, "Very much so."

Joe smiled and said, "The Lord be praised." Then he started breathing in gasps. Sam offered a small prayer for him and Joe said, "Amen." Suddenly, his eyes brightened up and he said, "I see the angels!" He then slumped over and was gone.

Amos Joe started crying and said, "Grandpa, Grandpa!"

They carefully laid him down on the floor and covered him with a blanket. Sam called Jacob; he said he would come right away. Soon Jacob arrived, as did several of the members. Sam, Martha, and the boys sat there and sobbed. Jacob offered a comforting prayer. Steven just happened to stop by and wondered why all the people were there. Sam met him at the door and gave him a hug then took him to where his father was.

Steven said, "I thought I was ready for this time, but this is harder than I thought it would be. We thought we were going to lose Dad when Mom passed, but the Lord knew we needed him for awhile longer. That was five years ago."

Sam said, "The encouraging counsel your father gave in those five years, if written, could fill a book."

Word quickly spread about Joe passing. Being in his upper nineties there were many folks who knew him. Most of them had fond memories of the counsel he gave.

Sam's folks and Uncle Ronald's came to the funeral. Uncle Ronald helped with the services. Sam's dad helped with the song starting. The church ladies brought in much food and helped serve folks who came. Amos Joe and James were happy to see their Grandpas, yet they knew Joe as their Grandpa too, so that was a confusing time for them.

Jacob and Ronald gave much encouraging thoughts on the resurrection of those who are faithful servants and die in the Lord. As the funeral drew to a close, Jacob stood up and said, "A few weeks ago our brother asked if we could sing a song that means a lot to him. It was a song that brought him peace during time of turmoil and storms. Today we know that Joe is not only listening to the angels sing, but is joining in singing praise in His presence. Please turn to hymn number four eighty-three." Soon the meeting house rang out with:

> *While I draw this fleeting breath,*
> *When my eye-lids close in death,*
> *When I soar to worlds unknown,*
> *See thee on thy judgment throne,*
> *Rock of Ages shelter me,*
> *Let me hide myself in thee.*

As they sang this last verse, Sam broke down and sobbed. His thoughts went back some twelve years ago, up on the hill behind their house by the old log, thinking he was a long way from anyone who cared, he had sung that song. That is when Joe had walked up the hill needing help. He remembered the experiences of those two days, how May was so sick and after giving her medicine and some supper she wanted to sing that song, how she had fallen asleep as the last line was finished. Sam remembered the following evening, how the church people had came and the young people sang to Joe's.

His mind went even further back to sitting on his mother's lap as a small boy. This was one of the songs they would sing. He thought about the girl who came to help Joe's during their sickness. The one who was faithful to them to the point she wouldn't leave them to have a friend from far off. These thoughts made the tears flow even more, and it was that girl sitting beside him now who was squeezing his hand to comfort him in this time of grief.

Then his thoughts went to the day May died. How she passed on just as they were singing the last line of this precious song. He remembered the times May told him this song was so comforting to her. Then he remembered times Joe talked of the comfort of the last days. He thought of how concerned Joe and May were for each other. How now, the wife God had given him was comforting him.

The house seemed lonely after Sam's folks went home. He was happy they stayed for a few days after the funeral. Steven came and got his father's belongings, except some of the furniture which he gave to them.

Sam was busy with his carpentry work as he had gotten behind over the last few days. Daniel helped where he could. That was good for Sam as he knew the adjustment would be hard. Having such a good wife was such a help. The boys were a help too, as their needs drew their minds to the blessings of a loving God.

Added Responsibilities
Chapter 17

A year after Joe passed away there was another adjustment in Sam and Martha's lives. They were blessed with the arrival of twin girls. Alice May and Amanda Fay were only five pounds two ounces and five pounds one ounce, but they were healthy little girls. Daniel's had taken the boys to their home for a couple of days. That delighted the boys.

June came to help Martha and brought the boys home to see their sisters. The boys were so thrilled when they saw them, they thought they were dolls. They were identical and so cute. Daniels came in the evening. Sam wanted his family together for the evening devotions, so Daniel and Amanda stayed for that, then took the boys and went home.

Sam put his arm around Martha and said, "The Lord took away two very special people from us and gave us two more very special souls."

She looked up to him with that special smile she had, "The Lord is good. Little girls are very close to their daddy's heart."

Sam was busy not only with the construction work, but with the ministry. He got called to preach funerals at adjoining districts and often took Jacob to official work when called.

There was a council meeting at their district one Saturday. Sam told Martha he didn't know of anything coming up, which perplexed him as Jacob usually talked over things which were to be considered. He said, "It surely isn't much." When they got to the meeting house, there were elders there from adjoining districts. Sam thought, "Maybe he went astray and they came to correct him."

After the opening service the elders went into the council room and asked each of the members to come through one at a time and answer the question asked of them. When Sam went through they asked him if he would submit to the voice of the Church. "Of course," he said he would. When they came out, they said, "This church has found Sam to be faithful in his calling as a minister and feels to ordain him to the eldership."

Sam's head dropped and tears fell to the floor. They called Martha to come to the front and stand by him. They were asked if they would accept this calling of the church and uphold the standards of this church and the scriptures. They answered in the affirmative. Then they were asked to kneel and two of the elders laid their hands on Sam's head and prayed over him. They asked the Lord to bless and guide him in the work of the Lord's Church. They were received into that calling by handshake and the holy kiss.

Jacob advised the members to let them go home and not visit them that night, as they needed the time alone with their little family.

When they got home, there was a dish of fruit on the table with a note that read, *"We knew you wouldn't feel like eating, but a little fruit may be helpful and the boys need something. Signed with love."*

Martha said, "We are not alone in this work, are we?"

Again it was the children who helped their parents reconcile to the change. As they were sitting on the couch reading from the Word of God, they heard something outside and opening the window it was clear. Up on the hill behind the house was the sound of some young folks singing *Rock of Ages.* Again it brought tears, tears of thankfulness. Amos Joe took hold of his hand and said, "Daddy, you can do it." and he looked up at him and smiled. What precious words.

At church the next day Sam received many encouraging comments. One of the visiting elders stayed and gave an excellent message of love from the Word of God.

With the new responsibility Sam was called to come different times to help in council meetings in other districts. Some of these were times he would like to stay at home, as there would be troubles in that church. At times like that he realized the more he knew the scriptures, the more fortified he was to help them overcome their troubles. He came home one time and told Martha, "If more people were like you, this world would be a better place to live."

Sam got a call from Josh that Margaret had passed away and asked him to come and preach her funeral. Sam told Martha, "In the days of the horse and buggy we wouldn't have heard of it until after the funeral." He asked her if she felt like going.

She responded, "Sure." The children were delighted so they all got in the model A and away they went.

They got there just as the sun was setting. Grandpa Amos was sitting on the porch swing and the boys went bounding upon the porch and into his arms. The twins came just as Alice came out of the door and both grabbed hold of her at the same time. She hugged them and gave each a kiss, then went to embrace the boys. As John and Mary came out with their children, Amos Joe went running to the car and brought the luggage in. Sam said, "Son, they haven't invited us to stay here yet."

Amos Joe said, "We are, aren't we?"

John said, "Why yes you are. Children help Amos take their luggage to their rooms upstairs."

Mary said, "We thought you would come, so I fixed a large pot of soup. Come on over and help us eat it." The boys thought that sure sounded good as it seemed a long ride over there. Mary said, "Come on over too Grandpa and Grandma."

As they all sat around the dining room table, John asked Sam to thank the Lord for the blessings they had. Sam looked at

John and said, "The years have gone by and there are so many changes taken place, would it be okay to have dad do that for us?"

John got tears in his eyes and said, "Yes," and, looking at his father, asked him if he would. Amos's voice was a little quivering, but the love he always had in his heart came forth in a very touching prayer. Alice went back to the bedroom and wept, thinking of the past and of the blessings of the present.

Alice May and Amanda Fay said, "Is Grandma all right?"

Martha said, "Oh yes, someday you will understand."

Sam was thinking of bygone days when he and John were boys, how back then they thought they were a happy family. Now years later, he recognized they truly are a happy family. "It is because we have parents who made the Lord the head of their home," he thought.

Sam's slept in the same room he had as a boy, and he remembered the times Satan was working on him. After all this time, he was still sorrowful for letting Satan lure him away from his father's house. He felt he must work to keep his children, and others, away from the clutches of the adversary, Satan.

The funeral was well attended with lot of tears. Margaret had several children and more grandchildren. This was a time of sorrow for them as well as for Josh. He said, "She was so much a comfort to me in my sun setting days after Mabel's passing." He asked Sam to preach to the living and not to the dead, as we have a hope beyond the grave.

At the funeral dinner Josh asked if he could talk to him after everyone was gone. He had a question for him. After a majority of the people had left and the rest were busy cleaning up the dinner, Josh and Sam found a quiet place to visit.

Josh said, "A family from another district wants to buy the farm and move into it. Sam, would you folks be interested in it?"

Sam said, "No, we are well established in our little area and church. What would you do?"

Josh said, "That is why I want your advice. They said I could just stay here and they would take care of me as long as I live. It sounds too good to be true. They have three small children, and this house is too little for that many of us. He wants to build on to it. Do you think that is a good idea, or even possible?"

Sam knew the house well and said, "Yes it could."

Josh said, "I want you to meet the family and explain the pros and cons of such a relationship. They are to be at your folks this evening so you can talk to them."

That evening, as they were sitting around the table, Josh came and soon Enos and Rebecca Wagoner showed up. They wanted to see Amos and Alice. After a little visit, Josh said he wanted Enos' to talk to Sam's a little privately. Amos said, "Go over to our place and we will keep the children." This must be the family Josh talked about, Sam realized.

As they all sat down around the table Josh got to the point. After laying the ground work Josh excused himself, "You folks talk; I'll go back over to John's."

Enos explained the plan they had. He and Rebecca knew about the years that Sam and Martha lived with Joe and May and wanted to hear the ins and outs of what could be expected. He said, "We know Josh and Mabel have no children, and feel it a Christian attribute to take care of those such as Josh. We have the means and want to buy it at a fair price, and let him stay there. When I first approached him he told me if he sold it, the swing would not stay, as Sam built it for him." Enos then told what they agreed on as the price. Sam thought that was a fair price.

Sam and Martha told them about the various things to expect, the sacrifice and the blessings they will receive. They shared how it is not an easy road, but is very rewarding. "You must have a very forgiving heart," Martha said. "Think about it as if you are working in the vineyard of the Lord."

Sam said, "The two of you must be in agreement on this, if so it will work. Josh is a very spiritual minded brother. You'll get lot of good counsel."

The next morning, after giving them farewell, they left for home. It was late when they got there, but they had an enjoyable trip, although it was a sorrowful occasion.

Another five years rolled by. Sam had been to many councils and Love Feasts. His family was such a help to him. There were many highlights and a few heartaches.

Some of the more memorable highlights were the times they went over to where he grew up to visit with his family there. Josh was now feeble and somewhat confused. He still had his faith foremost though. It was working out well for him and Enos'. There was a large room built on to the house and Josh got to keep his room. They added a bathroom close to his room, which he thought was wonderful. He said, "And to top it off, I still have my porch swing."

Sam got a call to go to his folk's district for some official work. Martha said as they were just over there lately she thought to stay home to keep the children on their school work. Jacob hardly went anymore, but wanted to go one more time. They met Josiah at a town along the way and the three rode over together. When they got there, Amos' were disappointed to not see the children, but they understood.

At the council meeting, the Elders said they thought it time to strengthen the ministry and the deacon office. This was brought before the Church and they were willing.

After the Church was voiced they came out, and Jacob announced they had called Enos Wagoner to the ministry, and John to the deacon office. It would have been Sam's responsibility to have installed them, but under the circumstances he asked to be excused. Jacob, although old and feeble, did it once more. It was touching to Amos and Alice to know their son was helping him and someday totally take his place.

Sam was so glad to have Josiah and Jacob along as they had such inspiring things to encourage those with added responsibilities. They came to Amos' after the meeting, and while Jacob and Josiah were visiting with Amos, Sam walked over to Josh's for a little talk with him. He was sitting on his porch swing and invited him to sit down. They had such a nice visit. It was apparent he was happy with their arrangement. The children came running out and called him Grandpa. He smiled when they did that. He said I'm so glad they came here.

Sam thought, "Enos is going to get good advice."

Jacob and Josiah were tired from a long day, the work they did was stressful. They asked to be excused and went over to John's and went to bed.

Sam visited with his folks for awhile and got some more advice from them. He knew what he got now he couldn't get after they were gone.

The next morning was a cloudy day, and it looked as if it would rain. Alice wanted to fix breakfast for them. She knew preachers didn't eat much before going to meeting. She had mush and sausage with coffee. Josiah offered a short, but inspiring prayer. Being rested up, they had a good conversation. They made it plain that they would open and bear testimony, but Sam needed to take the text. Sam didn't eat as much as the others.

Sam talked about the mountains in our life. He talked about Caleb and the mountain he wanted, where there were giants. He said, "Caleb knew it was bigger than he, but when God is with us there is no mountain too big. It's only when we put our trust in man and leave God out of it, we get scared of mountains. There were many people who could have entered into the Promised Land if they would have put their trust in God and then showed that faith by moving forward. God does expect us to do all he instructs. That shows we believe in him."

Jacob had opened, and Josiah closed with prayer and asked the blessing on that Church and their labors. After some visiting they went to Enos' for a dinner. That gave them some time to answer questions he had. Then they all went to John's for the night.

Mary fed them and Amos' a good breakfast and they were on their way home early. Sam wasn't sure about Josiah when they got to his car, but he said he was staying there for the night and going on in the morning.

It was late when they arrived at Jacob's place, but Jacob's wife was waiting up for him. Sam thought, "Just like Joe and May, concerned for each other. More people should be like that."

When he got home Martha was also waiting up. She met him at the door and said, "The children wanted to wait up for you, but fell asleep. James came carrying the Bible and said, 'Mommy, daddy would want us to read', and Amos said, 'And pray.' " Sam knew that while he was away someone from home was praying for him.

The Shepherd
Chapter 18

Jacob called and wanted Sam to come over. He had something to talk over with him. After Sam greeted Jacob and Merial, Jacob said, "Have a seat."

Sam was wondering what he wanted, when Merial came in with some tea for them. He thanked her, while still wondering what Jacob wanted. He thought, "Just be patient and you'll find out."

Jacob talked about the Church and many of the blessings he had seen through the years. He talked about the growth that had taken place.

He talked about the time an angel had sent Sam to help Joe and May. He said, "The things which have transpired over the years, have been proof that the Lord is working in this community."

"Sam, you and Martha have been such a good influence to the people here, and, although there have been some difficult situations, you have shown the way God wants His people to live. Sam, I'm now ninety-three years old and my strength has left me. I think it is time for me to turn the oversight of this Church over to you."

Sam said, "With my past life I don't feel I'm worthy."

Jacob replied, "I don't see it that way. Of course if you did feel worthy, you likely wouldn't be. The future of this congregation depends on its leadership. I think it's time to again strengthen the ministry, so you would have help."

Sam sat there contemplating their conversation. After a period of silence he said, "It looks like a mountain to me, but so did the Promised Land to the Children of Israel. Only if we are with the Lord will it work."

Jacob said, "It is that attitude that makes me think you can do it."

Sam asked, "You will still help in the giving of advice, won't you?"

Jacob smiled, "As long as the Lord keeps my mind working."

Sam went home and told Martha what Jacob wanted and she said, "We need to pray about it, as it is a mountain bigger than we are. Sam, you know I will support you as much as I can. Just remember the angel God sent to lead you all the way to your father's home and brought us together. He is still leading us as we work to bring these little children up in the nurture and admonition of the Lord."

As they had their evening devotions, Sam and Martha talked to their children about what could take place at Church council. They prayed the Lord's will be done.

At the council Jacob told the people what he wanted to do. He explained the fact of life was that he was old and not likely to be there much longer. That brought many tears as the members loved him. He was a father to them. They understood what he said about life and the need of keeping the Church alive. They were willing to move ahead with the work.

The adjoining Elders took the voice of the church and all were willing to relieve him of that responsibility, but reluctantly and with tears. They were willing to give that duty to Sam. The Church voiced to call Martha's brother, Raymond Jones to the ministry. Again many tears shed, as they were installed into their office.

Jacob stood up and thanked the congregation for their support that day and all the years he was their Shepherd. He turned to Sam and said, "Sam, you are now the Shepherd of this Flock. They will hear your voice as long as you cling to the Word of God with all your heart." Sam couldn't keep the tears from coming as he remembered the day he stood on the front porch of his father's house, as his brother had given him a ewe lamb. John had said he was giving him a ewe lamb from the best of the flock for a new start, that sometime he would have a flock of his own that would hear his voice. He felt the chills run down his back as he thought of the responsibility now on his shoulders. He knew it had to be with the help of the Almighty God.

There were many encouraging words given to Raymond by the Elders who came and by Jacob. Jacob told the congregation to let them have the evening to themselves and their family. "You can pray for them."

After Sam's got home, the thought of the new duty he now had hit him hard. He sat down and wept. Amos Joe, being a very tender hearted boy, came to him and sat down. Putting an arm around his dad said, "Dad you can do it, we will try to help you." Sam looked down and smiled at Amos Joe, "Thank you, son."

Sam visited Jacob's often for short visits. Jacob and Merial were so tired most of the time and didn't attend meeting much anymore. Sam felt like he was like Elisha when Elijah was about to be taken away. One of the last visits, Jacob told Sam to think about increasing the ministry to a plural body.

Jacob said, "There were only forty members when you came to help them and now there are over a hundred. With the young families there will soon be more."

Sam said, "That is a good problem to have. It's not the Lord's will that any perish, and neither is it ours."

Jacob said, "Amen."

Raymond and Julie came one evening wanting to talk about the ministry. Sam tried to pass on the counsel he was given when he was first called to preach. Martha had some advice for Julie about patience with Raymond in his work, as it is the Lord's work.

Sam was busy with his carpentry work and the Church took a lot of his time. He wondered if he was neglecting his family. At different times he would come home from work tired, and Martha would tell him a couple was coming over to talk to him after supper.

Sam didn't want to turn them away when he felt they were having marriage difficulties. If that was their problem he would ask Martha to be with him. She would always have good advice for the wife. Sam had a lot of experience with the Lord's teaching of forgiveness. He always encouraged them on filling their lives with the word of God. He told them marriage difficulty is the tool of Satan working, so fill your thoughts with godly things. It might be songs of praise to God. He said, "There is a saying, the family who prays together stays together, and singing praises is a form of praying. When inward feelings are sharp it may be easier to sing praises to God for awhile until you feel better. Then look each other in the eye and tell each other 'I forgive you.'" Sam remembered the time when John took him by the hands and forgave him. At that time hatred was conquered with love. He would tell them, "I've been there and I know it works." Sam and Martha would pray with those seeking advice. Sometimes they would sing with them, and when they did they got the children to come in and help sing. Seeing the children singing with enthusiasm would help the hurting couple understand the need to teach their children the love of a godly home.

Not all visits were hard, as the times when a couple came with a teenage son or daughter who wanted to be baptized. These were joyful occasions.

Two more years rolled by, and the labors of the Church seemed to increase. Raymond was doing well with his ministry. He was a real help to Sam, but having two children he needed time with them too.

Jacob and Merial had gone to their heavenly home, so he didn't have his council to help him. He talked to Daniel often, who gave him good advice. Sam's father told him they had the same problem some time ago, so the Church there decided to have the plural ministry.

Amos said, "They now have three ministers and three deacons. That gives them an official body to help with the work. It is working out well."

Sam talked this over with Raymond and with the deacon felt to talk to the Church about it. They had Council Meeting, and, after discussing the proposal, the voice was to put in another minister and a deacon. Sam said, "It is necessary to call in the adjoining Elders to take the voice." They appointed a council for in two weeks.

Uncle Ronald and Enos came along with Roy and Josiah from the adjoining district. After some encouraging thoughts on strengthening the church of God, they went into the council room and the members came through and gave their voice. When the Elders came out they said this church has voiced to ordain Raymond to the Eldership, and has chosen Peter Brubaker to the ministry, and Eli Brunk to the deacon's office. There were more tears shed. Raymond was installed in the usual order by the laying on of hands. The others were installed in the usual manner with handshake and the holy kiss. There was much encouraging remarks given.

When they went home Amos Joe came to Sam and said, "Daddy, you have help now, maybe you will have time to play with us sometime." That brought tears to his eyes.

Martha came to Sam and said, "The boys have been very patient waiting to play with their daddy."

Sam said, "I think my wife has been too."

The load was definitely lighter with the plural ministry. Sam still had folks come to him with their troubles, but several also confided in Raymond. If people had complaints they would consider it as a body and not alone. With more ministers, there was more time for the ministry to visit among the members which helped to bring closeness to each other.

Another two years passed by and the plural ministry was working out very well. The Church now consisted of one hundred and fifty members. With three ministers and two deacons dividing the work they had time for their families and to do other things.

Sam's liked to take their children up to the trail where the log was and have a picnic once in awhile. Amos said, "I would like Uncle John's to come sometime. We could have a picnic and maybe walk the trail for awhile."

Sam told him, "That would be nice, but there wouldn't be enough room for all of them."

Sam inquired about the land beyond the trail and found out it could be bought. He and Martha considered the cost and bought the twenty-acre parcel. They told their friends about the purchase and asked them if they would like to help clear off a flat area on the side of the mountain. They explained how it would make a nice picnic area. It would be available for the young folks and others who would like to take their families there to have an enjoyable day.

They got a lot of response, so work days were scheduled and were always well attended. Amos Joe told the volunteers the history about the log beside the trail. Some of the bigger boys said, "Why don't we replace it with a new one that is not decayed?"

James said, "Daddy sat on that log singing *Rock of Ages* a long time ago. That's when Joe came up and asked daddy to come and help them." When he said that, they started to sing *Rock of Ages*.

Martha and Julie, who was visiting, heard the singing. They came up to see who was there singing so beautifully. Martha had some tears well up in her eyes, as she thought of Joe's. She told the young folk boys history of the log that Amos Joe was not aware of. They asked if she thought Sam would care if they replaced it with a new one. She said she was sure he wouldn't care.

There were several work days as the young folks liked that hill and the trail. They even blazed a couple of trails on up the mountain. They took some fallen trees and made some benches and picnic tables. One of the boys took a log to the sawmill and had it split in half. Putting short legs on each of the log halves to keep them off the ground made two benches. He was handy with carving tools, and carved the complete song of *Rock of Ages* in the flat side of one of them. He then sealed them so they would last a long time. It took several of the boys to carry them up to the picnic area, but they got them there. Carefully, they removed the old rotten log and disposed of it. They placed the bench with the song where the old one was.

It was soon hiking season on the long distance trail that passed through the finished picnic area. Sam had just gotten home from work when Amos Joe came down the hill. "Hey Dad, is it okay for the hikers to get water from our spring behind the house? The big boys want to know."

Sam said, "Of course I don't care. Maybe we should fix it up better if others are getting water there." Amos Joe and James told the big boys their dad didn't care but thinks he should fix it up better if others are going to get water.

The boys cut a slab of a log and took it home and carved in it "Welcome Hikers – Spring Water". An arrow under the wording pointed down the trail to the spring. They sealed it like they did the log seats. After they had it secured in the proper place they asked the boys to get their dad. Sam and Martha, along with the girls, came up. They were impressed when they saw the log with *Rock of Ages* carved in it. Then they saw the sign and were pleased at what they had done.

Sam said, "You boys have done a wonderful job here. You have enhanced the beauty of God's creation and have made it known we feel to share with others these blessings. Concerning the spring I think we need to improve it."

One of the boys said, "You spend a lot of time being a Shepherd to us, and we would like to fix it up if you don't care. We think we can make it look nice."

Sam was touched and said, "Sure, you may."

Sam noticed the youth working up at the spring in the evenings, but didn't pay attention in particular. One day when he came home from work he happened around the house and was stunned at what he saw. There was stone work with a wishing well effect with water running out a trough, a place you could hold a cup or bottle to fill it, then running on over rocks with a rippling effect and on down into a tank where animals could drink.

They had laid a stone walkway leading up to the spring with shrubs along the sides, a couple of benches sat next to the beautiful landscaped spring. A carved sign hung above the bubbling pool said, "Living Water."

Sam told the young folks, "I am so happy with the work you have done. Tell your parents they are welcome to use the picnic area, as are all the young folks."

One evening as they were sitting on the front porch, they heard singing. It was so beautiful as they could hear both boys and girls voices. Most of the young folks must have been up there.

Martha said, "If Joe and May thought they heard the angels singing before, what do you think they would say if they were here now?"

Sam said, "What we hear is a foretaste of what they are enjoying."

The Trip
Chapter 19

Sam wanted to visit Eli and Abigail in Indiana. He could not get it out of his mind what those folks did for him and the sorrow about their son. He thought since they had three ministers and two deacons they could be gone for a while. He talked it over with Raymond and Peter and they understood his concern. Sam felt it best if they could take their family along. Martha's folks said they would look after things at their place while Sam's were gone.

Early on a Monday morning they got in their Model A and headed towards Indiana. Sam remembered the Model T he drove years ago and the difference now. He thought of the long trip home, and how much quicker it would be now. He said, "I sang a lot on my way home," and started singing. Martha and the children joined in.

Two days later they were close to Greenfield, Indiana. Sam wasn't sure just where the farm was, so he missed it. Suddenly he spotted the stream where he had spent the night and soaked his feet, years ago. He remembered the dream he had of his mother at the cook stove. It was here he found his little Bible that was so much help to him.

They sat along the road and tears filled his eyes as he thought of what might have happened. To the children it was just a little stream, but to him it was a place where he opened his heart to the Lord. They turned around and soon found the farm where Eli and Abigail lived. As they turned in he wondered if they were still alive, or if someone he never met lived there.

They pulled up to the yard gate just as an old lady came out walking with a cane. Sam got out and walked toward her with a smile on his face. She looked at him, with a frown and suddenly in an unsure voice said, "Sam?"

Sam said, "Abigail."

She turned around and said, "Eli, come!"

Shortly Eli came out and at first didn't recognize their visitor, but when Sam smiled he said, "I would remember that smile anyplace."

Sam introduced them to Martha and the children. Abigail said, "Come on in and sit a spell." They went into the house and Sam thought it looked just as it did the first time he was there. The same cook stove was still there. He remembered Abigail fixing him breakfast when he was so hungry. He noticed a large pile of split wood, where he split wood for them at that time.

Eli had a lot of questions and said, "We are sure glad you came. Would you stay a few days?"

Sam replied, "We would like to stay until after Sunday, if it is okay with you folks. Do you have room for us?"

Abigail said, "We do, that certainly would be nice."

Eli wanted to show him some things around the farm. The only livestock they had now were a few sheep. He said, "I must have my sheep," and he smiled. "The little lambs are so special, as they make me think of the teachings of Jesus in the Bible. He is the good Shepherd and we are the sheep."

Sam said, "Aren't we thankful to be sheep of his pasture?"

Eli looked at Sam and asked if he was walking close to the Lord now. He said, "By all appearance, I believe you are. Tonight after the children are asleep we want to hear of your experiences since you left here. We have had some you would be interested in."

Abigail fixed a large supper with the help of Martha and the girls. Martha said, "We are not big eaters, so you don't have to fix much."

The men walked out to the shed and fed the sheep. Sam said, "There is one that needs some medicine."

Eli said, "You know something about sheep, don't you?"

Sam said, "A little." Eli got the medicine and Sam held the lamb while he gave it to him.

A car came down the road and turned in. There were a man and woman with four children in the car. The man and the two oldest, which were boys, came toward the shed, while the woman and girls went into the house. Eli said, "Sam, I want you to meet my son Fred. Fred, this is Sam Wagoner." Eli then introduced his two grandsons, Rob and Chuck. Sam in turn, introduced his sons to them. The boys soon struck up a friendship and found they were close to the same age. This made Amos and James happy, as they had thought they were going to be bored not having anyone their age to be with.

As the women and girls entered the house, Abigail introduced her daughter-in-law Phyllis, and her granddaughters, Wilma and Joan to Martha.

The men went in the house where they were all introduced. Abigail said, "Come on into the dining room, supper is ready." Eli showed them where to sit and they bowed their heads while he thanked the Lord for their blessings. There was a large dish of fried potatoes and another of hamburger gravy along with bread and jelly.

Abigail said, "Sam, I knew you liked fried potatoes."

Amos thought, "I don't know how she knew dad liked them, but I sure do."

After they were finished, they all thanked Abigail and Eli for the wonderful supper. The younger girls said, "Now you ladies go in the living room and visit while we clean up the dishes and wash them."

Amos said, "We'll help you."

James said, "Sure we will."

Rob and Chuck weren't so sure they wanted to. James said, "Come and help, it will be fun."

They all started to clean up the table. The boys brought the dishes out while the girls started to wash. Then Amos began to sing *Rock of Ages,* and soon they all joined in. They sang song after song of the good ol' songs of Zion. When they were finished with the dishes, Rob said, "I didn't know doing dishes was so enjoyable."

As they went through the living room on their way to the porch they noticed Sam and Fred wiping their eyes. Eli and Abigail were red eyed.

On the porch the children enjoyed themselves visiting and playing some games. Occasionally there was another song heard. Come time for Fred's to leave, the girls wanted to spend the night together and the boys also did. The parents talked about it and it was decided the girls would go with Fred's and the boys stay there. That made for eight happy children.

After the boys were in bed, Eli and Abigail wanted to talk, so Sam told them the story of his life since he had left them. Eli said, "I sure wish we could have met Joe and May. We are so glad you came."

Eli hung his head as if deep in thought, then said, "About six months after you left our minister knocked on the door. I remember it as if it were yesterday. We had just finished dinner. His wife was with him and we invited them in. Considering the time of day, we asked if they had eaten. They said, 'Thank you, but we're not hungry.' They only wanted to talk. They had taken in a homeless boy, and as they were older thought it may not work out too well. They said, 'He came knocking at our door last evening just before we went to bed. We couldn't turn him away. He was cold and hungry. His clothing was ragged and dirty. We invited him in, fixed him some food, and gave him a place to sleep. We don't have any clothes for a boy like that, but we thought of you folks. We felt likely you still had some of your son's clothing. Would you be willing to let a homeless boy live with you for awhile?'"

"Sounds like your minister was testing your Christian resolve," Sam interjected.

"He was," Eli continued, "We looked at each other and thought about our son, how if he knocked at someone's door and was in distress, how we'd hope they would take him in. We told our minister we did still have some of Fred's clothes. If they fit he was welcome to have some. As for him staying with us? We decided to give it a try. Our minister excused himself and said, 'Thank you. I'll be right back.' Shortly he returned with a ragged young man. The boy was so thin he looked ghostly. As we looked at him, he started weeping, 'Will you let me stay?' He asked. We immediately recognized the voice. It was Fred."

After regaining his composure, Eli said, "Sam, the night you were here and getting ready to leave we prayed. Not only did we pray for you but also for Fred, and all others in that condition. You shed tears. We felt you would be guided into holiness and would be praying for Fred."

Sam said, "Yes, when you prayed for your son I realized my parents had been praying for me all the time I was gone. As I went on my way I knew you were praying for me too. That is the reason I felt I wanted to come see you. I'm so delighted to meet Fred and his family. Was adjusting to his return hard?"

"It was." Eli answered, "Not for us as much as for Fred. He had trouble forgiving himself."

Sam said, "I still struggle with that, but being born again I have faith the Lord has forgiven me."

Eli said, "That is what had to take place with Fred. We told him we forgave him and we feel he should forgive himself. It was the minister who worked with him and the deacon, along with some of the church members, that helped him see his need of a loving Savior."

"After he accepted Christ and was baptized he was a new boy. He started to go to the singings and soon was able to sing along with the rest of them. It was then that Phyllis came into his life and it was apparent she had no feelings against him. They had a pure romance and were married after two years. When at one time we didn't know if we would ever see Fred again, now we have wonderful grandchildren."

Sam said, "Prayer changes things, as we have a forgiving, loving God. We knelt in prayer when I was ready to leave. Now we know what the Lord has done for us, could we kneel together again, and you pray for us, we still need it."

Eli humbly said, "Yes." The four knelt in prayer while Eli offered a solemn, thankful prayer.

The next morning after breakfast and devotions, Eli said he had some work to do at the barn. Once the chores were done they would take Fred's boys home and pick up Sam's girls. Amos and James helped with the work and soon they were ready to go.

Eli said, "It's a little way over to Fred's place, but with the better roads now and the auto we don't mind going farther."

On the way to Fred's, Eli said, "Let me tell you about Fred's farm. A few years ago an old man started coming to church who nobody knew much about. He was reserved for awhile, but the members befriended him, and invited him into their homes. After a time he somewhat loosened up. He was a bachelor and had a farm just outside of Greenfield."

"One evening a group of folks were at Fred and Phyllis' for supper and this gentleman was there as well. He brought up that he was getting old and was considering selling his farm. That raised Fred's interest as they were looking for a farm. This pleased the man as he seemed to take a liking to Fred's children."

"One day the man came to Fred and told him he had prayed about selling the farm. It came to him that he would like to sell them his farm for a very little price. If they would let him live with them the rest of his life, he would give the farm to them. He said he was getting old and hadn't done the things he thought he should for eternal salvation. He said he had been selfish and greedy."

"Did the man ever come to the Lord?" Sam asked.

"Once he asked what was expected of someone who wanted into the church. Fred, who is now a deacon, explained things about following the Bible teachings. The man told Fred he had treated a forlorn boy very badly and not paid him what he was worth. He said the boy left and he didn't know whatever happened to him. He asked Fred, 'How I can repay this wrongdoing if I can't find him?' Fred told him to give to someone else in need or give it to charity and pray the Lord will forgive. Fred told him you know the earth is the Lord's and He provides for his own. If you do that you won't have to feel guilty."

"Did he ever repent and join the Church?" Sam interjected.

Eli said, "The man came into fellowship by Christian baptism and was a new person. He talked about how the boy he mistreated was so patient and never complained. That was what made him start thinking there was more to life than money."

Eli slowed for oncoming traffic as he continued, "Fred and Phyllis talked it over and thought to keep an old brother in his later days was a worthy thing to do. They told him they would take care of him but wanted to buy the farm. He was happy with their decision but was determined to give them the farm as payment for their assistance. Fred talked it over with the ministry and they felt it alright to accept it with the mindset, if they got into a condition they could help someone else in some way, they would."

"Fred's have been there for several years and things have gone well for them. They built an addition with an indoor bathroom onto the house soon after they moved there. The old brother became very sincere and read his Bible every day. He loved the children and as more came along he gave them gifts saying 'To my new grandchild.' The children dearly loved him. We feel he became part of our family. We were so sad when he suddenly passed away with a heart attack last year. One of the last things he said before he died was 'I hope the Lord has forgiven me for the way I treated that boy.' Fred assured him, as he had taken Jesus into his life he had nothing to worry about."

Eli turned north on the road out of Greenfield. Sam had been thinking the story Eli had been telling sounded familiar and asked, "Was that brother's name George?"

Eli said, "How did you know?" They were soon at Fred's farm and Sam recognized the place. He noticed there had been some needed repairs done and an addition had been added to the house.

Fred was in the barn tending to the livestock. The girls were in the house. Sam walked through the barn noticing the improvements that had been made, but still recognizing some things he remembered from years ago. He marveled how the Lord works in a mysterious way to bring to pass things we don't know about. He talked about how things used to be there and Fred and Eli wondered how he knew about those things.

Sam said, "The upstairs room on the north side was a very cold place to sleep without any heat in the winter."

Fred said, "You slept in it?" Sam nodded his head as Fred continued, "So, were you the boy George talked about?"

Sam replied, "I may have been, or there may have been another. I never felt I left a very good impression on George. If I was the one, I forgave him a long time ago. In fact I was thankful he treated me the way he did. It helped bring me to my senses. I've thought many times if he paid me well and I had acquired wealth, I may have gone on to Chicago. We all know that would have led to worse sins and I may have never found my way back home. Truly, all things work together for the good to those who love the Lord. My return was because of those who were faithful in praying for me. The Lord heard their prayers. Our children don't really know how blessed they are to have godly parents."

Eli said, "The suffering you endured here was just the start of better things to come." Adding to his fathers' comment, Fred said, "To think, that was what caused George to want to give the farm to us."

Sam said, "It was the wind whistling in that upstairs window, that made me decide to stay until spring. No matter how hard I had to work and how cold I got. The beauty of it all is, not only that Fred's got the farm, but that the hard shell of George was broken and he became a devout Christian. Also, that Fred's had the privilege of taking care of him in his latter days."

Eli said, "And to know how much the children meant to him, as he had no one. They were like his grandchildren."

Sam said, "Our God had this all in his hand and we are recipients of those blessings. Let's bow our heads in a little prayer, Eli would you lead us in prayer?" The boys were out playing, but the three men bowed their heads as Eli offered a touching prayer thanking the Lord for putting it in their hearts that brought them to this place in life and especially that one lost soul was saved. He ended the prayer with, *"May thy name be praised."*

As they came out of the barn, they heard a car coming and it turned in. It was Martha and Abigail in the Model A. Phyllis had called and invited them to come over so they could have a family dinner together again. That pleased the children. Eli said he would go in and rest a little before dinner. Sam and Fred took this opportunity to tell each other their story. They both agreed those were times of their lives they were ashamed of. They discussed how they could keep that from happening to their sons. They recognized, in no way were they blaming their mistakes on their parents, they felt to follow the example of their parents and try to be an example was the best they could do. God doesn't want robots, but each needs to from their own heart call on the name of the Lord.

They went in to a dinner of fried chicken, mashed potatoes and gravy, green beans plus pie. They sat around the table so richly spread with the good things to eat. Sam thought of the oat meal, turnip and occasional apple in the evening he had years ago. Back then, prayers were never said. Fred asked him to pray for them. With heads down he opened his mouth and thankful words of gratitude to God flowed out. To keep from breaking down, he opened his eyes up to heaven and let the praise flow. When finished there was a hearty, "Amen," by Eli and Fred.

After the meal and the thank you for the good dinner the men went into the living room and the children washed the dishes singing as they worked.

Fred said, "I am amazed what a difference it makes to the boys to sing as they work."

Abigail said, "We love to hear them singing."

Eli and Abigail wanted to lay down to rest a little, so the men went to the woods for a walk. Sam took Fred away back in the woods to a spring, where years ago they got water for the pigs in the winter when everything else was frozen. It was still there, but was hidden by weeds and it was soft all around as it hadn't been maintained for a long time. Fred was glad to know about it. He thought he could fix it up so it could be used again.

When they got to the buildings the children wanted to play ball, but there were only eight of them. They asked their dads to play with them. They said, "Okay, whose team are we on?" The children decided one on each team.

They were divided up with the oldest two boys and the oldest girls on one team and the younger ones on the other. Sam said, "I'll be with the younger ones."

The older ones were the first up, and they were doing good as the younger couldn't run as fast and were less experienced.

It was the last inning and the youngsters were behind three runs. The other team was comfortable they were going to win. The bases were loaded and Sam was at bat. He thought maybe he should do better than he had been doing. He deliberately struck on the first pitch. The second was a perfect pitch so he hit it away beyond the outfield and made a home run. That put them ahead of the older ones. That was a humbling experience for them.

Sam and Fred shook hands and said, "Good game." They told the children to do the same, so the boys shook hands with their brothers and the girls shook hands with their sisters.

Fred said, "It is good to teach our children good sportsmanship." When they went into the house the children told their mothers how much fun it was playing with their dads.

Eli and Abigail talked it over with Phyllis and Martha and it was decided Sam's would stay with Fred's that night and with Eli's the next night. That would give Eli's a quiet evening before Church the next morning.

Fred asked about the Church at Jeffrey, and when he found they had the plural ministry he took an interest. He said, "If we had that here, we could help more of the members with their difficulties and lighten the load on our minister."

Sam said, "I wouldn't want to try to change your customs, but it works well for our church."

After a good night's sleep they were treated to a small breakfast of toast and coffee or orange juice. They went to the church where Sam had been years ago with Eli's. He remembered the preacher talked about Elijah at the mouth of the cave and the tempest and the rending of the rocks, and then the still small voice of God.

Fred read the scripture the minister called for, after which the minister gave them an inspiring message about the way of God verses the way of man in his unconverted condition.

He invited Sam to bear testimony, which he very enthusiastically did encouraging them to a closer walk with God.

After meeting there was a carry in lunch served and much visiting. That was helpful to younger members wanting to hear from older brethren seasoned in the faith. After giving Fred's farewell, they went to Eli's for the evening and the night. Eli had a lot of things to talk about and it was hard to stop and go to bed.

Monday morning, they were up early, and the men went to care for the sheep. A ewe had twins overnight and the boys found it exciting to watch them wobble around. Eli said, "Just like newborn babes in the faith, they need some help sometimes. Soon they will be strong."

Abigail had a big breakfast ready when they came in from doing chores. They sat at the table and Eli offered a heart-rending prayer for them and others. After the breakfast was over and they had their devotions they gave them good bye and sang, *God be with you 'til we meet again.*

With mixed feelings they headed for home. Martha said, "Was this trip worth the time?"

"Very much so," Sam replied, "But yet I wonder about the flock at home."

Martha said, "What we learned here will increase our faith and fortify us to be better leaders of the flock."

The Campout
Chapter 20

Sam's arrived home in the early evening with a feeling of thankfulness. Although they were glad they made the trip, there is no place like home. The boys were happy to see the sheep and to find they were all well.

Daniel and Amanda came over to do the chores soon after Sam's got home. Martha invited them to stay for supper. She said, "The men have things they will want to talk about," and looking at her mother, smiled, "and we may too."

The years rolled by and Amos Joe was now a teenager. Martha felt it was hard to believe they had a son that old. One day he came to her and wanted to talk. He said he knew he was young, but he had been hearing in his mind as he lay awake at night a soft voice saying, "Come unto me." He said, "Mother, is it my imagination I hear that, or is God talking to me? I have felt for some time I wanted to be baptized, but I thought I was too young. It is a believer's baptism." He began to sob.

Martha put her arm around him and said, "Son, if you are old enough to believe the Bible, and are willing to walk accordingly, you are not too young. When Dad comes home this evening let's talk to him." She had to brush back a tear.

That evening after the children were in bed they asked Amos to stay up a little. Sam asked him about his dream and how it took place. He remembered the dream he had a long time ago. He thought if he had listened to the teachings of his father when he was young he may not have gone so far astray.

After Amos poured out his heart to them with tears, Sam said, "Son, we feel you are ready. You know the vows are made to God and are not to be broken."

Amos said, "Yes I know." Smiling he gave his dad and mother a big hug and went to bed. Sam and Martha wept with joy in their hearts that night.

The next evening, they went over to Raymond's and Sam said, "Amos has something he wants to tell you.

It was hard for Amos to get started, but with tears in his eyes, he told Uncle Raymond he wanted to be baptized.

Raymond smiled and said, "Praise the Lord. We had another come this morning with the same request, and Peter was here earlier with three others wanting baptism." The time was decided one week from Sunday after meeting. Amos was delighted to find out one of those was his very good friend who was only three weeks older than he.

The day came with the sun shining bright and a soft south wind blowing. Amos was happy as he had ever been. He was answering the call of the Spirit of the Almighty God, as were some of his friends. There were not only five, but seven, that felt to submit to their conscience and turn their lives to God.

All three ministers gave heartfelt messages on walking with God and the joy at the end of the journey. Raymond administered the baptisms. Afterward there was a potluck dinner. At the meal Amos Joe overheard one of the men say, "Today is the result of a very good shepherd leading the flock and they hear his voice."

A letter from Sam's folks arrived saying they planned on coming for a few days in three weeks if it suited. The letter said John's would be bringing them. The children were delighted.

Martha said, "Children you will have to work hard so you won't get behind on your schooling."

The twins in unison jumped up and down saying, "We will, we will!"

Martha was their school teacher and mother. She also felt the need to be a good shepherd of the lambs God had given them. Part of their schooling was how to crochet. The whole class made pot holders and little things, but she didn't have the boys learn larger things like afghans. Sam taught the boys woodworking, while the girls learned to crochet larger things. Martha made a lot of nice afghans, which she would give as gifts. Her mother had taught her at a very young age, and she liked it. The girls caught on quickly.

Sometimes, when Grandma Jones was there, they would all sit around crocheting as they visited. If the girls had trouble with something Grandma would show them how. By the time they were in the young folks they could make most anything with yarn and thread. Grandma said, "To learn young will be helpful when you grow old and can't work anymore. People really like gifts made by hand. There is a deep feeling in them."

Martha also taught the children to work in the garden. She taught them how to put the seed in the soil and to cover it up, then to watch as they peeped through the soil. She said, "This shows us the coming forth of new life."

One morning Alice came running in with the eggs mother sent her out to get, "Mother the peas we planted last week are coming up."

The children all went running out to see them. Martha came walking out. Sam, coming in from chores, noticed everyone in the garden and stopped by to see what the excitement was about. The children were so excited to see the peas lined down the rows. All five rows were up. James said, "Seeing this makes me sorry for the complaining I did, while placing those little seeds one inch apart."

Martha taught them all the things they planted. The new life of that little seed was so fascinating to them, as was the anticipation of a rewarding harvest.

There was plenty of rain and the crops grew well, but so did the weeds. One morning Martha said, "We need to hoe the weeds out of the garden." She took the children out and they hoed for an hour. It didn't seem as if they were getting far. The sun was so hot and the weeds were so contrary. When they complained Martha would say, "Remember the harvest, and the good food we'll have next winter."

When Sam came home from work he said, "After supper we are going to have some family time together."

The twins shouted, "Whoopee."

James, being a little more suspicious, asked, "What are we going to do?"

Sam said, "We are going to enjoy it, but wait until after supper and I'll tell you."

The children could hardly eat for the excitement of what they might do as a family. After the dishes were done they went out to the garden.

Sam said, "We are going to have a contest. We are going to see who can do the best job of hoeing and not complain. Speed will not be considered, but a good job will. The sun is behind the mountain so it won't be so hot. Mother and I are going to hoe too and not complain. Think of it as a family working together for a cause. Let's sing the first verse of *Jesus lover of my soul.* Then I'll tell you a story."

After the verse was sung he told them a story: "Back in the days of slaves, there was a boy stolen from his native country and brought to this land. He was sold on the auction block to the highest bidder. The man who bought him wasn't a Christian man and was very mean. He made this boy work hard in his field hoeing weeds all day long. If the boy didn't get as much done as he thought he should in a day, he didn't get any supper and had to sleep on the ground. When he did get supper, it was a cold piece of fish. The days were hot and long, and sometimes the boy got so tired he would lie down between the rows and go to sleep. His master found him asleep one day and kicked him so hard he could hardly get up. Then he whipped him with a cord, until blood came out of his back. By morning he was so sick with a fever the man was afraid he would die and he would lose a slave.

He gave him some medicine and put a shirt on him, so no one could see the stripes on his back. He took him back to the auction, hoping to get his money out of him."

"There was a man at the auction who could tell the slave was sick, but still bought him. The owner bid against him until he got his money out of him. The new owner took him home and cleaned out his wounds, gave him a good supper and put him into a warm soft bed. Before he left his room, he held his hand and prayed for him. The boy didn't know his new owner's language, but sensed his love. The man leaned down and kissed him on the cheek, and gave him a hug. The boy started crying. The man called his family in, there were twelve children and his wife, and they sang *Jesus lover of my soul*. The boy went to sleep as the last line was sung."

"After a long night's sleep he awoke wondering where he was. At first he thought he was in heaven. It was close to noon when he awoke and the wife brought in some clean clothes for him. She smiled at him and put her arm around him and kissed his cheek. When he came out of the bedroom there was dinner on the table. The family all came in and they bowed their heads as the father prayed. The boy couldn't eat much as he was not used to eating. The family all acted happy, something he hadn't seen since he was taken from his home. When the boy healed up he was glad to help the family in the field, as they sang *Jesus lover of my soul*. There was never a whip or a cross word. They did not work in the heat of the day"

"In time the slave learned their language and asked, 'Why did you buy me?' The man replied, 'Jesus bought me with his precious blood. Now I am free. I bought you to set you free.' The boy cried and gave the man a hug. He said, 'I love to work with your family, and to sing with them.' The man said, 'You may stay as long as you wish, but you are free to leave when you want.' The man said, 'I hope to see the day when all of the slaves are free in this country, but you better stay until that happens lest someone captures you and sells you again.' The boy never complained about going to the field to hoe, as he never had to go alone. In time, as they were singing, his voice was heard above the rest singing *Jesus lover of my soul*."

"After the slaves were freed, the boy was baptized and later became a minister. He did find his father and mother and were reunited with them, but he always called the man dad."

When Sam finished the story, the children were weeping, as was Martha.

Amos said, "Aren't we blessed?"

The others said, "We sure are, let's finish singing *Jesus lover of my soul*." As they finished the last note, they were finished hoeing and the garden looked beautiful.

Sam said, "Now for the watermelon I brought home." That brought more smiles.

After enjoying the melon, Sam said, "Now for a family doing something together; Friday evening we can take supper up to the campground and have a cookout. We can sleep there and have breakfast in the morning."

The twins put their arms around their daddy and said, "Daddy, you are so good to us." They placed a kiss on his cheek.

Friday evening was beautiful, and the children were glad to have so much fun. Their parents told them to invite friends to come for the supper, and if they wanted to stay overnight, to bring their sleeping bags. Martha's folks came for the evening meal. They all enjoyed sitting around the campfire visiting and singing. A few others came and helped with the supper and enjoyed the evening. The children had their best friends come and stay over.

The boys climbed the trail that went up to the top of the mountain. Just before dark they heard them singing, *How Great Thou Art*. The deep voice of those boys, along with the evening air was heart inspiring. It was late when Martha's folks went home, and some of the other older ones left. Sam and Martha set up their tent in the circle next to Martha's sister, June and her husband, Lester. The girls soon scurried into their sleeping bags on the one side of the circle and the boys on the other side. It was about midnight before Sam could be heard snoring.

Breakfast was not until nine o'clock, but it was another enjoyable occasion. There was early cowboy coffee and when all were up there was Bible reading, song and prayer, then breakfast of sausages and grits with eggs.

The time came to go home, and as they passed by, they smiled as they looked at the weed free garden.

The day finally arrived when Uncle John's came down the road in their thirty-six Ford. The car just came to a stop when out came the children, running to meet their cousins. John and Mary weren't as lively getting out as the trip made then somewhat stiff. They helped Grandpa and Grandma out. By this time the children had greeted each other and Sam's children all came running to Grandpa and Grandma for hugs and kisses.

Amos Joe said, "Come see our campground." He took them up to the log and shelter that the young folks built. Ray and Roy were thrilled with the place. They asked about the sign telling about the water and who the hikers it mentioned were. James spoke up and told them about the long distance hikers. The boys said they would like to hike sometime. Amos Joe said, "Maybe if you stay long enough we can go for a little hike."

The girls were looking at the log with the song of *Rock of Ages* carved in it. Alice May and Amanda Fay said, "That song means a lot to our dad." The girls said, "Let's sing it." They called the boys and they sang.

Sam invited the folks and John's up onto the porch and said, "Have a seat." Some sat on the two porch swings and some on rockers. As they were visiting, suddenly they heard someone singing.

Alice said, "Where is that coming from, it sounds like the children? Sam, I hear a voice that sounds like you did when you were young."

Amos said, "Isn't that beautiful? And more so as I feel it comes from their hearts." The singing gained strength when other voices joined in.

John asked, "Who is that?"

Sam replied, "You never know, as the sound echoes across the valley and folks like to join in on singing."

At the campground as they were singing along, a man and his son came down the trail. Dropping their backpacks next to a log they joined the children as they sang. The hikers knew the songs well and it was a reprieve to them. After a few songs, James asked if they needed anything.

The hikers said, "A place to camp for the night, and water. Mostly what we need is water. We didn't get as far as we thought we would. We were to meet our wives tonight, but are just too tired to go on without rest." The older man said if they had some way to call their wives they would have them come here, as this is such a beautiful place.

Amos said, "Come on down and get water. You may call from our phone."

The hikers were able to get a message to their wives so they planned to spend the night there. Amos Joe told them there were four boys going to camp there too.

After an evening with their family it was time to turn in. With the evening devotions finished, the boys said good night, took their sleeping gear, and went up to the camp site. The hikers were sitting around a campfire with their wives and two little boys. They said, "Come and join us." James asked about hiking and they told them about their hike and the joys of it and some things that weren't so good. They said, "This is one of the most joyful places we've been. How did this place come to be?"

Amos and James told them briefly about the history of the log and the time their dad met Joe and May. Then about how the church young folks fixed it up like it is. They wanted to know about the carving in the log. Amos explained it.

One of the wives asked, "Can we sing a couple of songs before we leave?" They all walked over to the log and sang *How Great Thou Art* and *Rock of Ages*.

Amos and Alice had been asleep, but they woke up hearing the singing up on the hill. As the notes faded away they went into a peaceful sleep. The wives of the hikers left and the campers crawled into their bags and fell asleep.

Early the next morning the boys were out of bed and ready to go down to the house to join their family for breakfast. Their hiker friends said they would be up and going by eight. They were just rousing when the boys were ready to go. The boys told the hikers to have a blessed day. The hikers responded with, "Thank you and God bless."

As the boys descended the path to the house, they talked about how there are a lot of good people in this world. James said, "Too bad some are not so good."

As they entered the house Martha asked, "Who would like to go to the hen house and get a dozen eggs?"

James said, "I will," as he bounded out the door, his cousins close behind. They returned soon with twelve large brown eggs.

Mary said, "Aren't we blessed to be on the farm where we have our own eggs, meat and vegetables?" Martha said, "Yes, and chores for our children that they may learn the value of what we live on."

They enjoyed a hearty breakfast of bacon and eggs with coffee or hot tea. After morning devotions, Sam said, "The children would like to have a cookout up at the campground and do some hiking on the trails. What do you think?"

Amos said, "Remember the time when Uncle Ronalds came and we went back to the pond? We had a very nice day with the cookout and walking thru the woods."

John and Sam said, "We sure do." The children were all ears as they talked about that day.

Amos, with a smile on his face said, "Alice and I may watch the camp while the rest do the trails."

Amos Joe said, "The children will carry the things needed up to the camp, and us boys will help Grandpa and Grandma up the path."

Alice replied with a smile, "That will be nice of you."

They had a wonderful day. The weather was pleasant, and they were happy to walk some of the trails. Amos and Alice enjoyed watching the squirrels scampering up the trees. Mary and Martha were content staying close to the camp, but they walked some short trails.

During the day a couple hikers came along, and Amos welcomed them to sit a spell and rest. He offered them a drink and some food. They were friendly and had some interesting stories to tell. Before they went on their way Alice asked if they needed anything. There were a few things they could use so she gave them almost more than they had room for. They told her hikers call folks like them "Trail Angels". Martha and Mary were just coming to the camp and heard the last of the talk.

Martha said, "That is what May, who lived where we live, thought Sam was the first time she seen him."

Sam's invited Martha's folks and family along with several of the church folks to come for the evening meal. They brought wieners and chips and some brought a freezer of ice-cream. They built a camp fire in the pit and roasted hot dogs, and ate potato chips. The boys came up with another freezer of ice-cream. After they were finished they sang until it was getting late.

Amos and Alice told their sons, "We need to retire, so we will go down and turn in."

Alice said, "There is no more comforting way to go to sleep than to hear your loved ones singing those good old songs of Zion."

John said, "I remember that from when I was a young boy." He gave his mother a hug. Amos Joe and James helped their grandparents down the path to the house.

The three days passed quickly, and it was time to bid farewell. These goodbye times were hard for Amos and Alice, as they never knew when it would be the last.

The Sermon
Chapter 21

Sam was very busy with his building work. Amos Joe, now eighteen, helped his dad most of the time. James helped some and the father/sons team was so enjoyable. Many times when Sam had to do work in the church the boys carried on with the carpentry work.

The twins were examples of their mother in helping older people in need. They enjoyed having the young folks, especially in the summer time when they gathered up at the campground. The young folks had blazed more trails on up into the mountains. One went to the top where, on a clear day, a person could see far into the valleys beyond.

The church was still growing and there were several newly married couples. The three ministers were encouraged as the families seemed to uphold the gospel truths.

It was Sam's time to have the main message. He and Martha talked about how things could change if the prosperity continued. Martha said to warn before slipping occurred, would maybe keep it from happening.

Sam said, "Yes, it was told to Ezekiel, if he seen the enemy coming and didn't warn them they would perish, and he would too. He was instructed to warn, in hopes to save them. We have such a good flock. We want to build a strong fence that can withstand Satan."

Martha said, "The only fence that Satan can't get through is to instill into their hearts the true love of God. *He that is within you is greater than he that is in the world.*"

Sam said, "It is such a help to have a good wife that helps me so."

She smiled at him and said, "Let the spirit lead."

On Sunday morning, it was time for Sam to speak to the flock. After all these years the butterflies still seemed to make their way into his stomach. This time was no different. He shut his eyes and quietly asked God to speak through him.

"Dear brethren and sisters and all present. Again we come together to praise our Heavenly Father and our Lord and Savior Jesus Christ. It makes my heart rejoice to see this building filled almost to capacity with people who want to praise the God of Heaven and earth. The past few years this church has grown as the Spirit seems to have free course."

"Not only is the Church prospering, but the economy is too. We must be very careful with our spiritual lives in these prosperous days, as that is a time Satan can lure us to sleep. In the Judges we read the account of the story of Samson, how everything was going his way in his mind, but he didn't listen to his parents. Little by little, Satan can blind us by causing all things to be fine for us and we just don't see where we are going, until it is too late."

"Samson actually laid his head into the clutches of Satan, by laying his head in the lap of one he thought was a perfect, lovely lady and went to sleep. He was blinded to reality, although he should have known after three times she said, *the Philistines be on thee Samson*. He became so blind he told her his whole heart and we know how sad that love story ended. How could that have been avoided? Should he never have told her the truth? Should he have taken her away from her people? What should he have done?"

"Man, when looking at things the Lord says no to and longs for them, becomes blind to the love of God, and closes his eyes to reality. Had Samson listened to his parents' advice he would never have gone to the uncircumcised to find a wife. With the prosperity we have among us today, we will have to work harder to keep our eyes on the Lord. Not letting the ungodly pleasures of the uncircumcised of heart, find its way into our heart. Lest we too become blinded to the truth."

"Boys, when you look for a spouse, what do you look for? Is it someone who stands in front of a mirror for hours to be sure she looks just right? Or do you look for someone who respects her parents and has time to visit the old and infirmed? Does she treat her brothers with respect? Remember, if you get married she will be your companion for the rest of your life."

"Girls, what do you want in a husband? Is it someone who just thinks of himself and doesn't care about anyone else? Or do you want one who will guide your family into the way of the truth? Life is a short journey and we have a home beyond this one. We have a home that is forever blessed, if we trust in the Lord, and make not provisions for the flesh, to fulfill the lusts of this life."

"We have wonderful fellowship now and I hope we can keep it. We know Satan is alive and well and he may also know his time is short. We have no persecution here at Jeffrey, and I hope it continues, but we must be on our guard against the devil. He has gone around as a roaring lion in the past, destroying the Christians. He physically persecuted them in the past, but couldn't destroy them. They only prospered more."

"Now we have an abundant and easy life with no resistance from without. Will this prosperity cause us to turn from the true God to serve idols? No, it won't happen suddenly, but it could by letting little things into our homes. Things that take the children's mind off the love of God, just a little bit at a time. A long time ago I was told a little, little, little makes a lot. When I was told that it was to encourage me to read a little in my Bible every day and if I did I'd get more than I ever knew I'd get. By the same token to neglect the Bible a little, little, little makes more than a lot. Why? Because it becomes a habit, so we miss it altogether and get more into the things of the world. Then what happens?"

"Although we think we see clearly, we don't know we have slipped away from the fullness of God. Jesus said he was the Good Shepherd and the sheep hear his voice. How are we going to hear his voice if we stray from the sheep fold? How are we going to stay in the fold? We must fill our hearts with the word of God. When we make that decision to follow Christ and are baptized we start a new walk of life and try to crucify the lust of the flesh. It is a constant battle, but the more we have the knowledge of the word of God in our lives, the better able we are to do so."

"We have a wonderful body of believers here. How can we be strong enough to ward off Satan if he attacks us? We have many children who haven't had time to toughen in to what may come. How shall we do? Parents, always have time to hear your children's concerns. Always have devotions and sing with them the old songs of Zion. Put the love of God in their hearts while they are young, and it will always be there. They may leave it, but it will not leave them."

"Have time to play with them. Teach them to be a good sport, even when they lose. Teach them the beauty of saying, 'I forgive,' and to not hold a grudge. To do this we as parents and grandparents must live that life. It is Christ in you, the hope of glory. Yes, it is so true we need to have our lives filled with the God of our salvation. Then we'll pray for each other, love each other, forgive each other, and help each other bear our burdens. May we ever be strong in the faith, looking for our Lord and Savior to come."

"The angel to the seven Churches in Asia found five of them lacking in some point. Are we like Ephesus? They were fairly good, but they left their first love. No, I believe the love of God is manifest among us. Smyrna was the poor church which suffered much persecution. They were told not to fear the things they endured, as Jesus would give them a crown of life. Pergamos had the doctrine of Balaam, which was to eat things sacrificed to idols and commit fornication. I believe we have a church clean of those things. Thyatira had preachers teaching fornication was acceptable. Sardis was not active in the faith, not watching the teaching of Jesus. Laodicea was lukewarm in the faith, neither hot nor cold, which was not good in the mouth of the Lord."

"These churches were given the privilege to repent of their deeds. If we are guilty of any of these conditions, we also have the privilege to repent. I see our church as the church of Philadelphia. He said he set before us an open door that no man can shut. He said we have a little strength, meaning we are mortal creatures, but we kept his word and did not deny his name. Because we kept the word of his patience, he will keep us from the hour of temptation that will come on all the world that dwells upon the earth. He said hold fast that no man take your crown."

"I want to emphasize we hold fast. We have a good Church and Satan will try hard to split it into pieces, but we have the Word, and, as we have been practicing the patience of Jesus, He will keep us from the pitfalls of apostasy. Sometimes we may suffer; Jesus did. Sometimes we may become discouraged; Jesus was. Sometimes we may be tempted; Jesus was. Sometimes our brethren may, so to speak, spit in our face. They did the same to Jesus. There may be other things happen that we think is not right, and it was that way with Jesus.

"Jesus, for the joy that was set before him, endured the cross, suffered the shame, paid the cost of sin and now sits at the right hand of God. Dearly beloved, let us keep on looking to Jesus, far above the sinful pleasures of this world, and he will make us a pillar in the Temple of God where Satan can't possibly harm us."

Satan at Work
Chapter 22

The Church continued to prosper. There were now over two hundred members and a large number of children. The meeting house was filled to capacity every Sunday. The ministry talked about what to do about it. There was a suggestion to build on or build new.

Sam said, "Our problem is a good one, but also a serious one. Sometimes when churches get this problem, Satan comes and the last is worse than the first."

There was a meeting with the members to discuss the options. A suggestion came forth to make two districts as several members lived over east a few miles. Peter lived over there, and could be their minister. Sam suggested they put it off for two weeks. He asked that they fast and pray during that time, that the Lord's will be revealed. The suggestion was seconded, so after a parting hymn and prayer, they were dismissed.

Amos, now nineteen, had started dating Ellen Smith. Ellen was the sister of one of his close friends, Matthew. Matthew was his age and Ellen a year younger.

Amos told his parents, "If we make two districts, Ellen will be in the other one. Will I not be able to date her?"

Sam smiled, and Martha said, "Son, your father asked me to court him when he lived in another state. Distance does not separate kindred spirits."

That evening, Sam and Martha talked about how they had grown close to each of the dear members. "Maybe we have neglected to feel the love of Christians at other places. There is nothing wrong with feeling close to those we go to church with every Sunday, but we must also feel compassion for those elsewhere."

James said, "Like over at Greenfield?" He had been writing to Rob and Chuck Gibson about once a month since they had been over there.

Martha said, "Yes and others too."

Sam said, "That is true, but we don't want to let a wedge get started into our love for the Lord. If we have two districts here at Jeffrey area, maybe we could let the light of the Lord shine brighter." That was the talk of most of the members for the next week.

Sam and the other officials needed to meet for some council. It was decided they would meet at Raymond's that evening. There were several matters to consider, so it took awhile. Sometimes they would just visit, instead of keeping on the subject at hand. That would make it take longer, but they enjoyed each other. It was about ten thirty when they were done and were ready to go home.

They walked out on the porch and noticed how bright the stars were. It was a pleasant night, with no wind, just a slight breeze from the south. Peter remarked about it being such a pleasant evening.

Raymond said, "It makes a person glad to be alive."

One of the deacons noticed there was an automobile in front of the church just to the west of Raymond's farm, and asked, "Who is at the meeting house at a time like this?"

Both deacons decided to walk over there and investigate. They were about half way there, when someone came running out of the church. Multiple gunshots shattered the quiet night. Cries of distress echoed through the hills as they witnessed three individuals running to the car.

Hearing the cries for help caused Sam, Raymond, and Peter to start running for the church. The car spun around spraying gravel as it came right at the men. It now appeared as if they had become the target. If it wasn't for the trees along the road, they may have been run over. The car sped away, but not before Peter got the license plate number.

Frozen for what seemed like eternity, yet only a couple of seconds, they watched the car speed away. The loud cries of pain brought their attention back to the church. As they crossed the road to the meeting house, they could see flames coming from an open door. The deacons were kneeling beside three boys lying on the ground.

They said, "They're gone!"

Raymond ran home and called the sheriff and the fire department. Already the fire was raging in the meeting house.

When Raymond returned he found Sam talking to three boys he quickly recognized were part of the young folks. Sam was trying to get the boys to tell him what happened. They were so shaken up and appeared to be in shock.

After they regained their composure, they started to explain, "We were up at the campground praying and fasting, with meditation in behalf of the church until about ten. We were on our way home, and as we passed the meeting house, we noticed the car with an Illinois licensed plate. That's when we seen someone in the church, and went up to see who it was. When we walked into the church, three tough looking men were pouring fuel all over the benches from five-gallon cans. One of them had just lit some straw on fire when the other two saw us and hollered. That's when we noticed they had guns. We ran out of the church and tried to hide, but it was too late as they started shooting. After they left we pulled the ones shot away from the church so the fire wouldn't get to them."

The sheriff and the ambulance came. They checked the three boys on the ground and saw that they were gone. They still loaded them into the ambulance and took them to the hospital. The Sheriff took the other three boys to the hospital, as he thought they may need some medical attention.

Peter said, "We should go get their parents and take them to the hospital."

Sam thought he should go home and tell his family what happened, as one of the fatalities was Amos' good friend, Matthew. As he was leaving he could see the flashing lights of the fire trucks and hear the sirens. The deacons stayed at the church while Raymond and Peter went to break the news, and the hearts, of three families.

When Sam entered the house Martha asked if the church is burning. He said, "The meeting house is burning, and the Church is being tried, but it will not be destroyed. Let's bow our heads for a little prayer." He prayed the Lord would help them all in this time of trouble. They sat around the kitchen table in the middle of the night and Sam told his family what had happened.

He laid his hand on Amos Joe's shoulders and said, "Son, Matthew was one of the three boys killed tonight." Martha put her arms around him as they wept. James and the twins were all weeping. Sam said, "Let us kneel before our Lord." In a circle facing each other on their knees, with their arms around one another, all together they prayed the Lord's Prayer while weeping.

Amos, after a while of sobbing, thanked his parents for instilling the love of God deep into his heart, so that at a time like this he could turn to God knowing he would receive strength. A response like that coming from his son in this time of trouble made Sam shed more tears. He remembered when they expressed their appreciation to their parents for what they done for them, his father would say, "Pass it on boys." Little did he know a time like this would come. God is good.

The next morning the police located the car at a hotel only ten miles away. A short time later the police broke down the door and found three young men still asleep. They were from Chicago, and the car was stolen.

It didn't take long under interrogation before they confessed to the crime. They were trying to become members of a gang and the requirements were they had to burn two churches and kill someone.

When Sam heard that he remembered how he at one time wanted to go to Chicago. How thankful he was that the Lord intervened. The Lord heard the prayers of his parents and others and stopped him. The hard winter at George Smith's was good for him. He wondered, "Just what kind of parents did those three young men have?"

It was mid morning when Sam's went back over to the meeting house. A large number of people had gathered around, looking at the smoldering ruins of the place where they loved to worship. The fire department said that by the time they got there it was too far gone to save, but they protected other buildings. The Ministry called a meeting at the community building to talk to them and pray.

Sam encouraged the members to turn to the Lord with all their heart and try to bring their minds closer to God. He said, "Read your Bibles, and trust the Lord will bring us through this. All things work together for the good to those who love the Lord. We will be holding services in this building until further notice. Please pray for the families of the three boys who gave their lives. Also pray for the three young men in jail."

After the meeting, Sam's went to visit Matthew's family. Amos Joe didn't want to go in, but Sam said, "Son, you need to come along. The family needs to see you."

As they entered the house, Ellen came to them and fell into Sam's arms weeping. She said, "Matthew had a strong faith and lived it. He was ready to go at a moment's notice."

The boys had divided up into groups with a few each day spending time in prayer and fasting. They felt it was something they could do in support of the Church, trusting the Lord would lead them into His will.

Amos said, "I was to be with the group tomorrow."

Ellen looked at Amos and said, "I think we should not be with each other for a little while until we get over this feeling."

Amos responded, "I agree, as Satan might use this time of emotion to weaken our resolve."

Sam said, "That is good thinking and it will let you be more helpful in strengthening our flock."

The three families decided to have one funeral for all three boys. There were two days of visitation. The church burning, and murderous tragedy made the news all over the country. Many people from all around came to offer their condolences.

The funeral, held in the community building, was filled to capacity. Outside people were standing around the windows and doors. Peter was given the responsibility to open the service. He had spent a lot of time at the hospital with the families of the three surviving boys. He had his heart filled with the love of God, or he would have broken down. His words pointed toward heaven where there will be no parting, no sin, no hatred, no temptation, and no sorrow. He had many words of encouragement. When he sat down he buried his face into his hands and sobbed.

Sam stood up behind the makeshift preacher's table. Looking out over the room packed with mourners, his thoughts went to the issue that led up to this moment. Was it the sobbing mothers? Was it the tears in the eyes of the fathers? Was it the red eyed siblings just trying to understand? Sam too had trouble keeping his composure. "The Lord has called our attention to the scripture, '*If this house of our earthly tabernacle were dissolved, we have a building of God, not made by hands eternal in the heavens.*' Our three young brethren spent their final thirty six hours on this earth in prayer and fasting, while in meditation on behalf of our Church. No doubt they are with the Lord. The others, who were spared, will no doubt want to carry on the work. Not only them, but all the young folks over the last couple of days have shown a desire to carry on the work that was started. They will not be alone as all of us will join in fasting and prayer as we implore God for His will."

"There are three young men who traveled down the wrong path to Satan's workshop. One that led to murder, and destroying a house of worship, where the people of God meet. There have been other meeting houses burnt in an effort to destroy the people of God. There have been others give their lives for the cause of Christ. What those individuals wishing harm do not know, is the building they burn is not the Church. The Church is in our hearts and not a building. We know that if it's the Lord's will, we can and will build another building. The question is, will we allow what those wicked boys did cause our church to dissolve?"

"Remember who we are following. Jesus said, '*Destroy this house and in three days I'll build it again.*' They thought he was referring to the Temple, but he was referring to his earthly body. Wicked men had him crucified on a cross. He said, '*Father forgive them, they know not what they do.*' He said, 'It is finished,' cried with a loud voice and gave up the Ghost. When that happened, the veil of the temple was rent in twain from the top to the bottom, exposing the Holy of Holies."

"They thought they had destroyed him forever, but in three days he arose from the grave. Not only he arose, but he destroyed the power of Satan and death. Jesus told them, '*I am the resurrection and the life. He that believes in me hath eternal life, and he that believes in me shall not see death.*' What death? We see here three young people who have died. They died to the mortal but not to the immortal. They are where we hope to be sometime."

"We must remember those who caused this sorrow. What have they got to live for now? They likely will spend the rest of their days in prison. Not only in a literal prison, but even if they repent, their deeds will rest on their conscience the rest of their days. We know nothing about these boys. We suppose they were just some wild boys from the city. Could it be that they came from a home of godly council? Could it be children who rebelled and left their home to see the world? They may have parents praying for them today. We don't know. We know, as followers of Jesus, we don't want to become bitter, but pray for them. Jesus did that for those who crucified him. Let us look up and trust the Lord will heal in time."

Raymond closed the service by giving much encouragement. "Do not stay here in this moment of time in your life, but look beyond and into eternal life. While we are here we must work to rebuild our Church and our faith in the love of God. Time will go on, so we want to be a stepping stone to some generation later who may suffer as we do."

Time does go on. The county came in and cleaned up the site of where the meeting house was. They continued to have meeting in the community building. There were ministers who came and helped them at times. Uncle Ronald came with Enos one Sunday. He was getting old and wasn't as perky as he used to be, but had some good council to give concerning the faith. Enos gave them a heartwarming sermon on going on unto perfection.

Sam got a letter from Fred Gibson with a check which was unbelievable. Fred wrote, "The farm has been paying well and as you know it was given to us. I have always wanted to do something for the Lord with the amount it would have cost us. Before George died, I tried to pay him, but he resisted. He told me then that if I ever got in a good financial way and wanted to do something, give it to a cause of the Lord. I heard of your loss of the meeting house and want to help. Please do not reveal the source of these funds as the glory belongs to the Lord. The earth is the Lord's and the fullness thereof."

When Sam read the letter, he shed a tear as he thought of George, "Rough, tight-fisted George, repentant born-again George, generous George; he didn't live to see what his money would do for a people of God."

Sam called a meeting with the officials to discuss the gift. Sam explained, "I am not to tell where the money came from. There are no strings attached."

They inquired of Sam, "You're a builder, do you think there will be enough to rebuild?"

Sam said, "Yes and some." They called a council meeting for the next Tuesday evening to discuss it.

The New Building
Chapter 23

When they gathered at the meeting an offer was read. One of the brethren on the east side of the members was willing to donate ten acres of land for a meeting house. That offer brought much discussion and many questions. He stated it had a lot of trees ready to harvest. Many of them were poplar, some ash and some maple. He stated the land was somewhat rolling with a creek at the back and to the side was a mountain with a seeping spring. He felt it could be harnessed to become a water supply.

The question came up, "Do we want to build two meeting houses or one large one?" It was suggested that decision be made first. The suggestion was seconded and was opened for discussion. After much consideration, they took a voice and almost all wanted to end up with two meeting houses. That would lead up to eventually having two districts. The main thought was to make room for expansion, room for lost souls.

With the dual meeting house plan approved, the next question was, "Do we want to build at the old site or over east first?"

Sam spoke up, "We ministers have been counseling many of you who have trouble reconciling with what we have been through. It's not a lack of faith, we as humans have to have time to adjust to the sorrow. I feel if we built on the east location first, we could have our own meeting house sooner, and as one district worship as we did before. That would help us to heal, and in due time we could build the west meeting house back where it was before. When completed, we will have overcome the devil."

Raymond spoke up and said, "Sam has expressed my mind exactly." Peter too agreed with them. The deacons also supported that thinking.

When the voice was taken there was a united mind to build over east first. They appointed a committee of three to look into the offer and bring back a report next Tuesday. Levi Smith and Amos Joe were on that committee.

The committee spent several days checking into things and the possibilities. The following Tuesday they brought back the report. It was a beautiful place. There were a lot of good poplar and ash trees, which could be harvested. Also several maple trees which could be left for shade. Off the road about two hundred feet was a nice knoll which could be a place for the meeting house and could have a basement with a walkout to the back. About three hundred feet east of the potential build site was the mountain with the seeping spring. The property was located on a country road, with very little traffic.

After the report was read there were a few questions, and then the voice was to accept it. They appointed a committee of five. The same three and two more were added. Amos Joe was the youngest, but he was the only one in the building business, so they felt he should be their foreman. He voiced that he could help with the construction, but there should be an older brother as foreman. They respected his feelings, so they voted Levi as foreman.

When Levi went home he told his family what happened and how Amos Joe, after being voted into the foreman job by the other committee members asked them to reconsider. He could help but he wanted to respect his elders.

Levi turned to Ellen and said, "He is a real brother, and if he comes back you should consider him."

The committee was careful to listen to what the members thought, and it was apparent they wanted to get things going as fast as was reasonable. They hired a logging crew to cut the trees they marked for timber and have them sawn into lumber. With the lumber stacked and drying, they hired a steam shovel to dig the basement. Two days later they were ready to start the foundation. There were a lot of volunteers to help with the concrete, so they got the basement walls and the floor poured in three days.

A neighbor in the gravel business volunteered to put in the drive. They told him it was a long winding drive.

He said, "I know, but that is no problem. I appreciated seeing things done in a nice workmanship way." He liked the way the drive wound through the maple trees back to the meeting house.

The word went out of when they planned to raise the building. There were people there from Virginia and Indiana, as well as from all the adjoining districts. Several neighbors came too. The women brought break and lunch. A lot of food and supplies were donated by others.

Amos Joe felt the pressure as being the one with the building knowledge. He depended on his father and brother to help him oversee the build. The workers were divided into groups and areas so it went well. The older folks brought lawn chairs and were the shade tree supervisors. Sam's were happy to see his parents there amongst the lawn chair folks. Amos was pleased to see the skill of his grandsons in the knowledge of building. John's and Enos' family were among the throng of volunteers that day.

Sam said, "This is just like a large family reunion with so many of our kin and the dear members working together in love."

Amos said, "It is apparent the love of God has not been diminished here, no matter what Satan did."

So many came that some went to Sam's wood working shop and built the benches. After two days the structure was up and roofed with the doors and windows in.

The three ministers thanked those who were so kind to come and help. Sam also took time to express to their dear members the faith they had shown in the way they worked together. God's work must go on. There were tears shed.

Over the next few weeks there were some more work days to finish the trim and paint. The benches also needed finished and put in place. It was an impressive sight the evening the wagons came in with all the benches. It was a steady line of brethren and boys carrying benches into the building. It kept the deacons busy telling them where each bench went.

Peter came to Sam and said six of the young folks came to him and wanted to be baptized. Matthew's brother and sister were among those requesting to join the Church. The ministry talked it over with the deacons and the building committee. They thought that although not everything was done, they could use the building.

Sam asked the deacons, "What about the creek?"

They walked back there and after looking it over, felt with a little work it could be made useable. They sounded it around and on Saturday several men came and before noon there was a beautiful place fixed to baptize.

When Sam's got home, their children were very quiet. As they ate dinner they would hardly eat.

Martha asked, "What's wrong, you're not eating?"

James said, "I would like to be baptized tomorrow."

Alice May said, "Me too."

Then Amanda Fay said, "I would like to as well."

That stopped the desire to eat more, as Sam and Martha were so encouraged to hear that from their children. Sam talked to them about the seriousness of vowing to God and the need to be faithful. Each of them said they had been praying about it for some time and felt they couldn't wait any longer.

Martha said, "We don't have time to make new dresses for you girls now, but I might have some old dresses that would fit."

They responded, "We would rather have the new life and the gift of the Holy Spirit than any new dress."

Sam said, "With that attitude you are ready." Sam contacted the officials and informed them. They were happy with the news.

Sunday was the first time to hold meeting in the new meeting house. It had been six months since that dreadful night. Sam said, "What a happy occasion to be back worshiping in our own house. Add to that happiness, the joy of having nine new souls added to the fold."

The ministers divided the preaching time. They didn't want anyone to say it was someone special to have the first sermon. The twins heard someone say, "Sam is sure a good shepherd, very kind and considerate of the sheep."

After the service they gathered at the creek where Sam, Raymond, and Peter administered the rite of baptism to the nine. It was a very impressive service, and a wonderful start.

A Blessing
Chapter 24

It took another six months of work until the landscaping and sidewalks were complete, along with small details in the building. They continued to use it during this time. It seemed that most of this work was accomplished on Saturdays. One of the first things they did was drill into the wall of the mountain where it was seeping and water flowed out. They drove a pipe into the hole and had a flowing fountain of pure water. They thanked the Lord for this life sustaining blessing.

When the project was totally finished the committee had their last meeting, and felt it was time to dissolve. In the beginning it looked like a larger job than they could do. The Lord helped them through all difficult situations. There were no serious disagreements between themselves through these labors.

Levi had been such a good foreman, with always a positive attitude. He said, "We started our first meeting with prayer, and I feel we should finish with prayer."

They bowed their heads while he offered a beautiful prayer, thanking their Heavenly Father for the help and blessings over this time. Levi prayed that the Lord would continue to bless the dear members as they work in His vineyard. He prayed for those boys in prison, if not against His will He would soften their hearts. When he said, "Amen," they all said, "Amen." Then, looking at each other, they joined hands in a circle and together prayed The Lord's prayer. As they were ready to depart they saluted each other with the Holy kiss and handshake.

Sam and the boys were busy with their building business. The load had been heavy on James as Amos had to spend time with the building committee. Sam spent much time with those who lost their sons. He also spent time at the prison visiting the boys who had committed the crime. They were hard hearted and wouldn't look him in the eye. He felt they must surely be possessed with evil spirits. He remembered how he at one time wanted to go to Chicago where all the pleasures were. To think he might be one of those behind bars. Many times he thanked the Lord for godly parents who were praying for him. "These boys may not have that, so we will pray for them," he thought.

After a year passed since the tragedy, Amos wrote to Ellen asking for her friendship in a special way. He didn't have to wait long before a letter came accepting his desire. They enjoyed their time together with their families. They especially liked to go up to the campground and watch the wild life. They would spend time cleaning up fallen limbs and other maintenance chores. Sometimes hikers came along and they enjoyed hearing tales from the trail.

They had been dating for a year before Amos asked for her hand in marriage. She accepted, so they started planning a wedding. When they talked to Levi and Opel they seemed happy to have Amos as a son-in-law.

Levi asked, "Could you build a house for me before you get married?"

Ellen and Amos talked about the wedding, and she said, "I would like to have a wedding like your parents had."

Amos questioned, "You mean after a regular church service?"

She said, "I feel that there is no better way and it would do away with all the ado some people go through."

Amos was a little surprised that she wanted one like his folks had, but he was in agreement if her parents were willing. They said, "Where would be a better place?"

Ellen asked Amos, "How long will it take to build a house?"

He smiled a little and said, "If that makes a difference, I might put someone on the back burner for awhile." They all laughed.

Amos and Ellen went over to Sam and Martha's and told them about the wedding plans. Ellen, smiling, looked at Martha and said, "We plan on having a church wedding like you had." Martha was delighted to think they were following their footsteps.

Sam and Martha asked, "When is this going to be?"

Amos said, "I don't have to work seven years, but I do have to build her folks a new house first."

Sam said, "Son, if you do it all by yourself, after your regular work, it may take fourteen years."

Ellen giggled and said, "And get the wrong girl? No way! I'll see to it that won't happen."

They chuckled a little, then got more serious and talked about how it could be accomplished in a reasonable time. Sam said he and James could finish the job they were on, so Amos could start the one for Levi.

Levi showed Amos where he wanted the house built. It was only one mile from the new meeting house. There was eight acres with some trees. Amos asked Levi who was going to live in their old place.

"We aren't planning to move. I just want to build a home with hopes someone would like it," said Levi.

Amos was surprised that Levi would build a home to sell so close to the new meeting house. Surely, he would sell it to some members.

With the other work, Amos worked as hard as he could to get it done. He often thought of Jacob when he was working for Rachel. Because of Jacob's love for Rachel, the fourteen years seemed but a short time. He thought, "The last six months seem to be a long time." Finally, the house was finished, and he gave the keys to Levi.

Amos and Ellen would spend as much time as they could in the presence of each other but not alone. They wanted to be sure to keep their courtship pure. One Sunday afternoon, they talked to Levi and Opel about when they thought they could get married.

Levi said, "The house is finished, so whenever the two of you want. Having it after Sunday service, it can be anytime."

Ellen and Amos looked at each other and smiled. She said, "In two weeks?"

Opel replied, "If you want."

Amos asked, "Where will we live?"

Levi said, "You can live in our basement until you get a place. It is all furnished." They decided in two weeks they would get married if the ministry were okay with that date.

Amos and Ellen talked about whom they would have marry them. They came to the conclusion to have Sam and Raymond preach the wedding sermon and have Peter perform the ceremony. They talked to Sam, and he thought it was a good plan.

They sent out some invitations to their friends and family explaining the wedding and how it was to be conducted. John's came and brought Sam's folks with them. They stayed at Daniels, as Amos wanted to have his family at home together one last time. It was a touching time when Sam read the scripture and they discussed it. They sang together and then prayed.

As they drove back the lane into the church parking lot Amos thought of the hours he had worked there to get the meeting house built. He thought if his friend Matthew were still alive, they would still be going to the old house. "We don't understand the plan of our loving God, but we trust he does all things well."

Although the new meeting house was bigger than the other one, it was still filled to capacity. Amos' cousin Enos came, but uncle Ronald's were not able to travel.

Amos and his Mother and siblings sat in the front row on one side and Ellen with her family sat on the front row on the other side. The grandparents filled in.

The ministers gave such encouraging talk about the love of God and his plan for the family. They spoke about how God sometimes takes our loved ones away to be where he is, but expects us to continue on. They talked about the home and the need for forgiving, trusting, and shouldering our responsibilities. The meeting was closed with hymn and prayer.

Sam stood up and announced there was a couple wanting to be married that day and all were invited to stay for the wedding and the dinner in the basement afterward.

Peter arose and asked Amos and Ellen to stand. He talked a little to Amos about his duties as husband, and to Ellen about her duties as wife. He then talked to both of them about their duties to their God. After joining right hands he performed the wedding vows.

They then had their first kiss. Peter asked them to kneel in prayer, their first prayer as husband and wife. After they arose, he introduced them as Mr. and Mrs. Amos Wagoner. Amos senior hugged his grandson and wept on his shoulder. Alice wept some, but as she had early stages of dementia, she wasn't what she used to be.

Levi and Opel gave them a big hug and said, "Amos, you now are our son."

There was some singing as family and friends congratulated Amos and Ellen. Then they moved to the basement where the newlyweds enjoyed their first meal as husband and wife with their friends and family.

There were several gifts. The girls brought them to Amos and Ellen to open. They got several useful things. The last gift was a large envelope. In it was a deed to a property and a card that said, "The house you built is yours. You worked so hard and long for no pay, building the meeting house, so Mother and I, along with several members, have given you this property. May God bless you two as you raise your family in this home." It was signed by Levi and Opel.

Amos broke down and cried. Ellen also shed many tears. Through the tears they said, "Thank you." When Amos got his composure he said, "I only wanted to be a servant to our God."

Sam and Martha, with John and Mary, encouraged them to keep working for the Lord and some time they could help someone else. Sam thought of the time John gave him a little lamb saying some day he could have a flock of his own. The love of God goes on and on.

Levi handed the keys to them with a smile on his face and said, "Amos, here are the keys you gave me after you finished the house. Now they are yours to keep."

After thanking everyone the young couple decided to walk to their new house, as it was only a mile away. Sam's, Levi's and John's walked with them. Daniel's drove the grandparents, as they were unable to walk that far. As they were walking down the lane of the meeting grounds the friends were singing, *God be with you until we meet again.*

Amos and Ellen walked onto the front porch. Amos thought about how many times he walked onto that porch wondering who would live there. He was glad he didn't know it would be him and his new wife. He put the key into the lock and opened the door. They both gasped as they found the home filled with furniture. A card lay on the table which said, "This furniture is our gift to you two from Dad and Mom Wagoner, James, Alice May, Amanda Fay, Grandpa and Grandma Wagoner, John and Mary and children."

Martha's parents and siblings, Peter and Ellen Brubaker and some others were there and together said, "Welcome home."

Grandpa Wagoner said, "Let us all bow our heads in prayer." He offered a lovely prayer in behalf of the new home just beginning. He asked for a blessing on Amos and Ellen as they labored for the Lord. Sam and John had some tears as it was such a deep sincere prayer like they knew him to pray when they were boys at home. They knew he was getting old and feeble, but his heart was deep in the love of God.

The new couple walked through the house looking at the furniture and all the things that were there. They could hardly believe what others had done for them. They stood in the living room with their arms around each other. Amos Joe said, "How can we ever pay you back for what you have done?"

Sam and Levi put their arms around their children and said, "Don't ever try to repay, just labor for the Lord and you likely will do for others more than we did for you, before you leave this world."

It was time to bid goodbyes. Sam winked at Ellen as he said, "Son, I know in the old law when a man married he didn't work for a year, but remember we live in the day of grace."

Ellen smiled and asked, "Could he have a week off?"

Everyone chuckled, as Sam replied, "We will try to get along for a week without him, but I doubt you can."

She gave him a hug and said, "Nope!" After everyone left Amos and Ellen went into the kitchen and found the refrigerator and pantry stocked with food.

Another Empty Chair
Chapter 25

Sam and Martha adjusted to not having Amos at home. Life has its changes. One evening after the children were all in bed, they were sitting on the porch swing discussing the changes since Joe and May's days.

Sam said, "Someday we'll be like they were when we got married. Life is a one way journey, but the end is glorious if we have the faith they had."

Suddenly they heard someone singing *Rock of Ages* from on the hill. Who could that be? They didn't have to wait long as Amos and Ellen came running and laughing down the path. They had gone to check on a job, and on the way home, decided to stop in a little. They thought it would be fun to sing a little before coming down. It was after dark and the sound had carried well. It was pleasant to hear. Martha invited them to sit on the other swing and she would get them a glass of ice tea. Amos said that sounded good. They didn't stay long, but it was enjoyable for them to stop for a few minutes.

After they left Sam said, "As we get older we'll like these visits more." The next morning the twins complained because they didn't get to see them.

The new meeting house was working out well. It had been three years since the first meeting. In this time there were eleven more baptisms. The Church was growing. After Amos and Ellen's wedding in the meeting house, other members thought that was so nice that, over the next three years, four more weddings were held at the church.

The ministers talked about the need of rebuilding the old meeting house. There were some of the older members living close to where it was, who wished they could go to Church there.

The officials discussed it and decided to call a council to see what the members thought.

There were several different views expressed of the advantage and disadvantage of two districts. The question was brought up about the finances. The deacons reported that they now had more than half enough to rebuild.

When the voice was taken, the majority was to start a building fund and as soon as there was enough to go ahead and start. They appointed a building committee of five brethren. Daniel Jones was the oldest and James Wagoner was the youngest. The committee chose Daniel for their foreman.

James was concerned about the work on the committee. He was close enough to what Amos had to do and he wondered if he could live up to what his brother did. He asked his father for a few days off as he said he had fish to fry in Indiana.

Martha told Sam, "He's been writing to Wilma Gibson for more than a year."

James asked, "Do you mind if the twins could go along."

Martha said, "One may, but I need one to stay here to help me."

James and Alice May left for Indiana in his forty one Ford early one morning. It was a big day, but they got to Indiana before dark. Alice noticed Wilma seemed extremely glad to see them. They had a nice visit, and soon it was time to think about bed. Fred called his folks and they said it was fine if James came over for the night. Abigail was glad to see him. She asked about his father. She said James reminded her of Sam.

The next morning James wanted to go early and have breakfast with Fred's. When he got there, Alice met him at the door, and said, "Are you?"

James smiled and said, "Maybe."

Alice couldn't believe her brother had been writing to Wilma for so long and she didn't know it. She said, "Well after all, you are twenty-four."

Before they left on Monday, it was decided there would be a wedding in six weeks. Alice May wasn't there when that was discussed, so she didn't know anything about it. James didn't say anything to her, but he noticed Alice May and Rob eyeing each other. The trip home was uneventful, and they got home before dark on Monday night.

Sam remarked, "It sure is closer with the cars now and the better roads."

After the twins were in bed he told his folks about his and Wilma's wedding plans. Sam said, "You had better work hard the next six weeks."

James worked hard trying to get ahead enough to take some time off for the wedding and awhile afterward. He tried to find a place to rent, as he wouldn't have time to build something for a long while, being on the building committee. Amos told him his father-in-law offered to let James and Wilma stay in their basement for a time, until they could find something. He knew what it was like being on a building committee.

James called Wilma and she thought that was kind of them. She was willing. James talked to Levi and they came to an agreement on price and conditions. Wilma liked the idea of the wedding in the meeting house, but their minister said it would be an innovation for them and he preferred not to.

Wilma said, "With the church out of the question, I would like to have a lawn wedding."

Her dad said, "You can use the new pole barn for a backup in case of rain."

That sounded fine to all, so the place and time was decided. Wilma asked, "Who will marry us?" She thought James wouldn't want her minister, as he didn't want them to have it in the church house.

James said, "I'm not a bit offended for your minister's stand on that. He is doing what he feels is his responsibility. If you would like to have him tie the knot, maybe dad could have a little talk before the ceremony."

Wilma said, "You're so easy to get along with James. That's why I love you."

James replied, "That is the way my parents and the Lord taught us."

The next few weeks were busy ones, but the time soon came to go to Indiana. Amos hired Ellen's brother Lloyd to help in the construction as they were getting more work. He wanted to learn the carpentry work and asked Amos if he could use him. It looked like that could work out fine. It would help catch up with the work they had promised.

The day came and so did most of those they invited. The weather was perfect for an outdoor wedding. James and Wilma wanted the congregation to sing a couple songs, Christian songs that everyone knew. Sam had the sermon, and then Wilma's minister Joseph, had the wedding. It was a nice one, although simple. Fred and Phyllis were tender, but happy their daughter was marrying into Sam's family. Eli and Abigail were delighted to have Sam's son as their grandson.

Phyllis said, "I am going to miss her."

Sam's missed James at the supper table every night, but it was nice to have them to come home at times. The girls looked forward to the evenings when Amos' and James' came. Martha would fix a large pot of soup and they would have some dessert the daughters-in-law brought. Sometimes they would play games and sometimes sing. There were always experiences to share.

Eight months after the decision to build, the deacons came over and told Sam they had enough funds to move ahead. Amos called a council meeting to inform the members. The building committee presented three plans, and after much discussion, they chose one. This was done by eliminating one and then voicing on the other two. A large majority chose one and the rest of the members said they would submit to that decision and support it.

Sam thanked them, saying, "Now we have a united mind to build and trust the Lord will help us in this project. May it be to the glory of God." It was turned over to the building Committee to go ahead.

Life Moving On
Chapter 26

The Committee moved ahead with the building project with enthusiasm. They hired an excavator to prepare the grounds. They were not going to have a basement as the committee found there to be spring water to deal with. The older members didn't want steps. So the plan the church chose was one with everything on the same level. This made it simpler and more cost effective.

There were several work days until the building was up and under roof. James' skill was such a help for those who were not used to carpentry. All they needed was someone to show them how to do it.

Although there were only periodic work days, James spent a lot of time with other church building related issues. This cut into the amount of time he could work with the construction crew, which made their income a little short.

James said, "It will all come out, as the Lord always provides for his own."

Sam opened his wood shop to build the benches. There were plenty of volunteers to help. They were made after the pattern used for those in the east house. The benches took some time to build and finish, but by the time the meeting house was ready, they were all done.

The members did most everything. It took a year to finish, including the landscaping. They didn't feel the pressure, having the east house to worship in.

James' were happy to live in the basement of Levi's house, although it was a little unhandy traveling over to the building site. An advantage of not being too close was that people didn't bother him as much in the evenings.

Sam was sitting on the porch swing one evening, watching the sun dropping beneath the trees, when Peter pulled in the drive. He said, "Sam, I think we need some help in the ministry. Now that there are two districts and we're having meeting in both places each Sunday."

Sam said, "I expected that to happen."

There was a council meeting on a Thursday evening at the east district. The Elders came. After the congregation was told what Peter wanted, the voice was taken, and it was a united voice to strengthen the ministry. After reading the scripture and some talk by the Elders, the voice was taken again. It fell on Amos and Ellen Wagoner. The Church received them into the office of the ministry. There were many encouraging remarks.

Sam told Amos, "Son, always trust in the Lord and give him the praise for the strength to proclaim the word." He remembered the counsel Jacob gave him years ago when he was called to preach. Sam told about the minister whom people thought was good, so someone asked him, "How do you do it?" And this is what he said: "It takes four things. First, study yourself full. Then think yourself clear. Then pray yourself hot. Then just let go." Sam said, "It takes all four and the last will be the hardest to do. Don't try to be someone else, just be yourself."

They also put in a deacon at the same time. The church was growing.

Sam heard their neighbor, Charlie, west of them by a mile was going to sell his farm. Sam went to him and asked about it. Charlie said after his wife died last year, he had trouble doing his own work, both at the barn and in the kitchen. He really didn't know what to do.

Sam said, "Would you consider selling it to James and Wilma?"

Charlie answered, "I don't know of anyone better." They set a date for a meeting with James' and Sam's.

James and Wilma thought it would be nice to have an eighty acre farm, but how to get it was something they didn't know. He had been saving for most of his working days, but to buy that much was beyond their means.

Sam said, "Let's see how much he wants?"

When they met with Charlie, he was happy to know they were interested. They asked how much he wanted for it. He told them what the going price was, but if one of the brethren wanted it, the price would be lower.

James said, "We are interested in it; if we can come up with the money."

Charlie said, "If you can come up with ten percent I will sell it on contract with no interest."

After doing some pencil pushing, the down payment was revealed. James and Wilma looked at each other and smiled, "We have enough to do that."

Charlie said, "The next problem is: where I will live?"

Wilma said, "Would you mind living with us? You can have your bedroom and be part of the family."

Charlie choked back some tears, "Do you really mean it?"

James said, "She sure does. My folks lived with Joe and May in their latter days."

Wilma said, "I too grew up living with an old brother in our home until he passed away. He was a Grandpa to us children, and he treated us like we were his grandchildren."

Sam said, "To keep older people in our homes is a blessing for both the aged and the younger. It takes some adjusting, but we know it will work."

Wilma said, "We can arrange for you to have some privacy."

Three weeks later, James' moved into Charlie's house. They built a bathroom adjoining his bedroom. This gave him the comforts of not going through the house to the bath. He had his place at the table with them. He was included in the family worship. He could hardly believe the blessings which he now enjoyed.

Charlie asked, "How can you do all this for me?"

James said, "We are brethren in the vineyard of the Lord. We would not want you to go to a nursing home."

A year after James' were married Alice May came to Sam and Martha and told them she was ready to get married. Sam acting as if he was surprised raised his eyebrows and asked, "To whom?" Her wry smile back at her father turned to seriousness as she explained how much she and Rob Gibson were in love.

Martha asked, "Where will you live?"

Alice May replied, "We plan to live close to Greenfield, Indiana."

Martha said, "Won't you miss us?"

Alice May said, "I know I will, but we feel the Lord is leading us this way."

Sam asked, "When do you plan on this wedding?"

"We would like, if it is O.K. with you," Alice May responded, "to be the fifteenth of May. We want a wedding like you had."

Being the early part of November, Martha knew they had time to prepare for a wedding, but to prepare to lose one if her daughters was a different thing. It wouldn't be so bad if she was going to live close, but her moving all the way to Indiana was something she didn't want to think about.

As Christmas time was approaching, Sam said, "Martha, I think we should have the family together for Christmas."

Martha said, "We need to see when James' are going to Wilma's folks. No doubt Phyllis misses her daughter and more also since little Rachel was born."

Amos and Ellen now had two boys, Dan and William. James and Wilma had recently been blessed with the arrival of a little girl. Sam said, "It is different with three grand children. It gives grandma something to do, right?"

Martha said, "Yes, but they are so sweet."

Two weeks before Christmas Amanda Fay told her mother she and Oscar Lavy were planning a wedding. Martha was shocked and sat there quietly as her mind was racing.

Alice May broke the silence, "We plan to have a double wedding."

Amanda, hoping to get some sense of approval from her mother said, "Don't you think that will be nice mom?"

Martha finally spoke up, "Amanda, do you plan to live close here?"

Amanda smiled, "Yes, we do."

Martha was glad to hear that and sighed with relief. When Sam came home, the girls wasted no time telling him.

He said, "It will be for life, so be sure you know what you're doing."

Later that evening, when Sam and Martha were alone, he told her, "Oscar was one of the boys we counseled after the tragedy. Even though it will always leave a scar, I do feel he is over the adverse effects of that night."

The Wagoner family did come together on Christmas Day. They had a large roasted turkey, mashed potatoes with gravy, and four kinds of pie. Martha didn't have to do much as the girls and daughters-in-law did most of it. Sam filled the candy dish, which almost never happened. They sang Christian Christmas songs and played games. There were some gifts, but before they opened them Sam read the account of the birth of Jesus in the Bible, then they knelt in prayer. Afterward they opened their gifts while Sam passed the popcorn and apples. The candy dish was being visited constantly.

Martha had told James to invite Charlie, as he didn't have anyone to be with on Christmas Day. Charlie had been reluctant at first, but by insistence he finally submitted. The smile on his face told them he was enjoying it. He was given a little gift which made him shed a tear.

The day was too soon over and it was time to bid goodbye. Martha said, "If the Lord will when we meet next Christmas there will be two more of us."

James said, "Or three more."

Ellen said, "Or four more."

Sam said with a smile, "When will this end?"

Amos replied, "Remember what Uncle John said when he gave you the little ewe lamb about someday having a flock of your own?"

They all laughed, and Sam said, "Seriously, I feel Mother and I have been well blessed to have a day like today."

Charlie spoke up, "You sure are, and I too have been blessed to be included in this joyous day where love abounds."

The men were glad when Spring came, as building in the winter is not always pleasant. Martha wasn't as enthused as usual, knowing the nest would soon be empty.

May came in pleasant with scattered thunderstorms and balmy air. This was the time of year one could feel glad to be alive. Flowers were coming out and the farmers were plowing their fields. The birds were happy, the trees had leafed out, and it was time to plant the garden.

The girls had helped Martha with the early garden, and were now helping plant the rest. They wanted to know why as much as normal was being planted, considering there would be only the two of them.

Martha smiled and said, "There will always be someone to help eat it."

As they planted, they talked about the times gone by when their whole family worked in the garden together singing and listening to stories dad told. Alice said, "Those were good days." and Amanda agreed with her. Martha let a tear fall from her cheek.

The wedding day came. Uncle John's came and brought his folks. Enos' brought Uncle Ronald's, although they were hardly able to travel. They wanted to come one more time.

Rob came two days before and stayed with Oscar. He stopped by for a visit and found Sam sitting on the porch swing watching the clouds growing in the west. Oscar joined his, soon to be, father-in-law.

"We will be staying around for about a week after the wedding," Rob said. "My folks moved into Grandpa's house to help them, as they are not able to care for themselves anymore."

Sam asked, "Are they still able to recognize people?"

Rob answered, "Yes they do. The folks are bringing them to the wedding. They are anxious to see you."

Peter canceled meeting in the east district for the wedding. There was a very large gathering as families from both boys were invited, besides all who normally gather for worship. They opened the doors into the dining area to make more room.

The girls wanted their dad to tie the knot. The wedding being after regular meeting, Peter opened and had prayer. Fred read the scripture called for. Enos took the main part, but left plenty of time for Raymond to bear testimony. He left a little time so Uncle Ronald, though he very seldom exercised any more, gave some very touching thoughts, then closed with hymn and prayer. Peter announced that, considering a number of out of state ministers were in the area, an evening service would be held at the east district that night at seven o'clock.

Sam stood up and made the announcements then said, "Today we have two couples who want to get married. We invite all to witness this sacred ceremony and stay for the dinner which will be at the conservation building."

He asked the two couples to stand. He gave each of the grooms instructions about their duties as husbands. He also gave the brides instructions as to their duties as the weaker vessel to support their husbands. To all of them he explained their duties to uphold the Biblical instructions of the home, and the Church, in prayer and reading the Bible. He talked about loving and forgiving each other. Then he asked Rob and Alice to join right hands and he asked them the questions of the wedding vows. They said, "I do." Then he turned to Oscar and Amanda and did the same, and they answered the same. He then turned to Rob and Alice and pronounced them husband and wife, then to Oscar and Amanda and pronounced them husband and wife.

Sam then said, "What God has joined together let not man put asunder. Let's kneel in prayer." He offered a deep, touching prayer for both couples. Raymond closed with the Lord's Prayer. Sam stood behind Rob and Alice and introduced Mr. and Mrs. Rob Gibson and they kissed. He then stood behind Oscar and Amanda and introduced Mr. and Mrs. Oscar Lavy and they kissed.

Someone started singing, *Blest be the tie that binds*. Sam sat down beside Martha, dropped his head in his hands, and sobbed. Martha put her arm around him and gave him a squeeze as tears were running down her cheek. The Grandparents congratulated them while Sam was getting his composure. Then Sam and Martha also gave them their blessings, with the groom's parents following.

At the dinner Sam got to visit with Eli and Abigail some. Eli was a little confused part of the time but not too bad. He asked Sam what he thought about his daughter living in the house where he lived with George Smith a long time ago.

Sam said, "I hope under different conditions. I hope there is better heat in the winter and better windows."

Eli smiled and said, "A lot better. We're so happy to have your daughter as our Granddaughter."

Sam said, "God is good."

Sam and Martha went home to an empty house, put their arms around each other, and wept. They thought of the day they came there after they were married. How Joe and May told them of days past and their ups and downs.

Martha said, "Remember how we went on the hill and sang Rock of Ages before we came down?"

Sam said, "I sure do remember."

As they remembered that joyous time they heard someone singing, *Rock of Ages* up on the hill. Sam said, "Our children."

Soon they came down the path, all four of them with their spouses and the little ones. They said, "We knew you needed something to bring a smile on your faces. So we thought to do this now, so you won't be shocked when we do it again years from now." Amos' and James didn't stay long as they needed to get to the evening service.

The evening meeting was well attended. Amos was surprised to see his folks and Uncle Ronald's there. Also Eli and Abigail were there with Fred's. Sam expected they were hoping to hear Amos Joe speak. Enos must have been thinking the same thing, as he left plenty of time at the end of his message. Uncle Ronald opened the service with the thought of faith. Enos took the text and talked about the vapor of our lives from the fifth chapter of James.

When it came time to close, the pressure was put on Amos, so he slowly got to his feet and softly began to speak. As he went on it seemed as if he couldn't let it out fast enough. It was apparent he had been filling his heart with the words of the Bible and now was letting go. You could feel the Holy Spirit working in him. Amos senior thought of the little ewe lamb John gave Sam in hope that someday Sam would have a flock of his own. He felt the Lamb of God is still in the hearts of his children and grandchildren and others who heard their voice.

Fred's had to get back as it was corn planting time and without Rob it was more work for them, so they left early

Monday morning. Wilma thought it was not fair, but James told her they'd try to go to their meeting this fall.

Enos' left on Monday as well taking Uncle Ronald's home. On Tuesday John's left for home with his folks. That was a sad goodbye for Sam, as he felt his folks were soon going to cross over.

Sam said, "When the sunset days come to loved ones it is not as if we have no hope, but to know we will not see them here again makes us sad."

The day came for Rob and Alice to say goodbye and it was harder than Alice thought it would be. She put her arms around her mother and wept for a long while. Martha wept too. After a while Martha said, "Remember you felt it was the Lord's will."

Wiping a tear from her eye Alice replied, "I still feel it is and I have no regrets, but the parting is still hard."

As the car went out of sight Martha said, "Now I know how Phyllis felt when Wilma left home after they were married."

Sam said, "Time does move on, as God intended it."

The Empty House
Chapter 27

With all the children gone from home, Sam and Martha had some adjusting to do. When they had gotten married they lived with Joe and May. Martha remembered the adjustment it took, and May also had needed to adjust to someone else in her kitchen. Now the house seemed so lonely and empty.

Sam said, "We are still able to help others, but in time we won't be able to go anyplace or do anything."

Martha said, "We have things to look forward to, such as when the children come home. Maybe we should go visit old people who can't get out."

Sam said, "That is a responsibility." Visiting the elderly was something Sam and Martha did even when their children were young. Time moved on and with it changes came.

Sam was busy with construction, working with his sons. When there were cabinets to build, he usually did that, as he liked working in the woodshop better than on the job away from home. Martha liked having Sam working at home, as he would come in the house to eat lunch. Martha also enjoyed the days Amanda came over. Some days Wilma came with little Rachel who was now a toddler.

Wilma needed a mother to talk to when she had low days, so Martha was the listening ear. She said, "Things are working well with Charlie living there, but he sometimes kind of gets on my nerves."

Martha said, "Yes, I know and sometimes you just have to bite your tongue. In the end the Lord will bless."

Wilma replied, "I try to and most times I do, but at times I feel I offend him."

Martha asked, "Does he have a forgiving spirit?"

Wilma answered, "Yes he does, but sometimes he goes to his room, and I hear him in there sobbing. When that happens, I wait until James comes home and I tell him about it. We go in there and I apologize and ask him to forgive me. Then he cries and says, 'Oh! Yes, I'm sorry to be so sensitive, I just miss Thelma so much.' James, bless his heart, then puts his arm around him and gives him a hug and says, 'We love you Charlie, and so does the Lord.' The last time that happened, Rachel came in and asked, 'Is Grandpa alright?' Charlie, with a smile on his face, picked her up and put her on his lap, giving her a squeeze said, 'Yes I'm okay.' She said, 'Love you Grandpa.'"

Martha said, "I believe you are doing well with the trials that have crossed your path, but at anytime you need someone to be a listening ear just come on over. I know you miss your mother and she misses you, just like I miss Alice, but it makes it easier when we are all the children of God."

Wilma said, "Yes and a God that understands our trials. Charlie really enjoys our times of devotions."

Martha smiled at her daughter-in-law, "I'm glad you have those times. Some folks don't."

It had been a year since the twins left home, and Sam hadn't seen his folks in that time. John wrote they were failing and he and Mary were living with them, as they couldn't care for themselves anymore. He said, "Mother's mind is getting worse. She keeps calling for you. It seems as if she thinks you are still gone, as when you left home as a young man."

Sam told Martha he felt they should go to see them soon. The boys said, "You go, we'll take care of the work. Now that we have Oscar, working full time, and also Lloyd, we will be alright." Sam and Martha packed up and left for Virginia.

When they got there Amos and Alice was so glad to see them Alice wept some, but she was having a better day. During their visit she looked at Sam and said, "Son, remember the day after you came home, we were making applesauce, and what an enjoyable time we had? How you opened up to me and told me all your heart? We spent that whole week together and I'll never forget it. Well, I want you to go down in the old basement and to the shelves on the east end. On the very top shelf you will find a jar of applesauce. It is the only one we have left from that day we canned. I have left it there to remind me of the joy that filled my heart with thankfulness to have you home again, and with love in your heart."

The creaking door hinges reminded Sam of years gone by as he made his way down the rough sawn steps that had not changed. Sure enough, there on the top shelf, covered with dust, was the jar of applesauce he placed there a long time ago. He knew the fruit inside wasn't good anymore, but the thought was precious. He stood there weeping, thinking of his mother's prayers. He left it there thinking he might want to look at it again someday.

Back upstairs and mother said, "Did you see it?" He said, "I sure did." And he gave her a hug, and then put a kiss on her cheek.

She said, "I told John not to use it or destroy it." They had a good visit and had supper together.

Alice said, "Son, they tell me you have been a good shepherd to the flock where you live, and they hear your voice. That now there are two flocks where there used to be one and your son is ministering to the other."

Sam said, "With the Lord's help. Praise His name."

With John and Mary living there, there wasn't room for Sam's to spend the night. John's son, Roy, and his wife were living in the main part of the house with their five children. So it was decided they were to stay at his cousin Enos' for the night. Enos was on the porch swing when they got there, so Sam sat with him, while Martha went in the house. Sam said in more of a statement than a question, "The old swing still holding up."

Enos replied with a grin as he looked at Sam, "Yes, it was built by an expert."

Sam chuckled and said, "Maybe it hasn't been used much?"

Enos replied, "Not enough. Nope! Not enough."

They had a good visit about bygone days, then about current events in the Church, and in the world. Enos told Sam about changes in farm practices since he was at home. Sam asked Enos what his thoughts were about the welfare of Sam's folks.

Enos said, "Your mother has her good days and her bad days, but the bad days are getting more frequent all the time. Your dad has lost his strength, but his mind is good. Your brother and Mary are doing super taking care of them."

The next day Sam walked around the farm a little with John, and of course things had changed, but he remembered some things. They walked back to the pond and talked about when Uncle Ronald's came and the day they spent there. As they were talking, Enos joined them, and they reminisced about bygone days.

Sam said, "Life is a one-way street, and we only have one chance to serve the Lord."

Enos and John in unison said, "Amen."

The next day as they took the parting hand, Alice was having a bad day, and she couldn't understand where they were going. Sam gave his mother a hug and said, "Remember the applesauce we made?" She sort of smiled and said, "Sure."

As they were going down the road Martha said, "It is hard, isn't it?"

Sam was silent for a few moments then replied, "It is, as we may never see them again. But it is looking beyond that sunset that helps us carry on. We still have work to do."

Toward evening they arrived home. When they walked from the car to the house they heard someone singing up on the hill. They sat down on the porch swing listening to such beautiful music. Martha thought she heard some children singing. Then they got up and went in the house and there was a sign hanging, which read, "Welcome to the lonely home." The table was stretched all the way out and plates were all around on it.

The door opened and in came Amos Joe, James, and Amanda with their companions and children. Sam and Martha were glad to see them but thought it might be more appreciated another time after they had some rest from their trip. Martha noticed the table stretched so long but hadn't counted the places set. They just finished greeting each other when there came a knock at the door and in came Alice May, Rob and their children. It was a little overwhelming for Sam and Martha and they had to sit down. Alice May gave her mother a hug. The girls started to bring in the supper as they all sang, *When there is love at home.* Martha just had to cry, and Sam couldn't keep from shedding some tears.

It was a good supper and everyone was interested in the news from Grandpa's. Rob and Alice planned to spend the night at Oscar and Amanda's, but they were all planning to all be together in two days for a family gathering. The twins said they would come over tomorrow. Rob wanted to go to work with the crew. They didn't stay long as they knew the folks would be tired, but before they left the house was in tip top shape. They had a family worship time together and then they were out of there.

Sam and Martha said, "Wasn't that nice." They were soon in bed, where they fell asleep to the sound of singing coming from up on the hill.

The next morning Sam, his sons, and sons-in-law all went to a house they were framing. It was a nice day to frame and the work seemed to fly. Sam said, "Those boys can climb around on a house like monkeys."

They told Sam, "You stay on the ground and be the saw man."

Lloyd had been helping long enough to know what to do as well as the rest. Rob was the only one not familiar with the work, but as a farmer he could do most things. They had such an enjoyable day. Part of the time they were singing, part of the time just talking, but most of the time working. By the time that it was time to pick up the tools, the tar paper was on.

That evening Sam told Martha, "The boys sure seemed to enjoy the day, and I did too."

The daughters and daughters-in-law were over by nine and the grandchildren went running to Martha saying, "Grandma, Grandma!" They all wanted hugs and kisses. Dan and William played with the tractors while Rachel played dolls. Amos' baby Paul was just starting to walk a little and wanted to get into everything. He kept Grandma busy, besides holding James' little six month old baby, Steven.

They had a busy and enjoyable day, sewing, fixing food for the next day, doing odd jobs for Martha, and just visiting. Martha thought, "It is not lonely now," as she looked at the happy family.

The predawn glow awoke Sam and he looked at Martha who had been awake for a while. He whispered, "It's quiet now, but wait a little and it will be different." Then he chuckled.

She said, "Yes, and we'll love every bit of it. Aren't we well blessed? How many lambs do you want in your flock?"

Sam said, "As many as the Lord sends us. I just hope they all grow up to have the Lamb of God in their hearts."

Sam read the first Psalm and they spent time in prayer. For breakfast all they had was a cup of coffee with a piece of toast, because they knew there was a big dinner coming later in the day.

The first of the family arrived at nine and by ten they were all there. Charlie came along with James' as he was just part of the family now. He never had children, so he enjoyed being included.

There was a lot of reminiscing, and laughs. The in-laws learned things they never knew before. Rob said, "We sure married into a happy family." Oscar agreed with him.

Charlie spoke up, "You're right about that."

At noon the ladies set a very enticing meal on the table. When they all were seated around the table, they sang a verse, and then Sam offered prayer. As they were eating Sam thought, "This will soon be over, and this room will be lonely again." Then he corrected his thoughts, "We are blessed, not only today, but every day, with the Church family and the freedom in this good land. We can worship as we know is right, the bountifulness of this land, all this and the Lord too. There is nothing to be sad about."

After eating a bountiful meal, the children brought in a freezer of ice-cream. They stayed through the evening, but the little ones took naps, and so did Charlie. Even Sam had a twenty minute nap.

The evening meal was a free for all. Anyone could have anything they could find. There was plenty of leftovers plus another freezer of homemade ice-cream. Sam popped some popcorn. At about four they sang for a while, which was enjoyable.

At about nine o'clock James' left for home. "Tomorrow is Sunday and we need to rest, so we don't sleep in church," James chuckled as he left.

Amos said, "If you preach you won't sleep."

Sam said, "It does make a difference." They all smiled.

After the boys left, the twins, with the help of their husbands, put the house in order. They knew if they didn't, their mother would before she went to bed. The door shut after the last one left and the house was quiet. Sam said, "Let's go to bed. Tomorrow is another day."

The Sunset
Chapter 28

Life goes on with its changes. Some are good and some are not so good. Sam's had gotten used to living in an empty house, however Martha was one that liked having company for dinner on Sundays. Through the week she spent time going to her daughter and daughters-in-law helping where she could. She enjoyed the grandchildren. From the time she was a girl she had helped those who needed help. She remembered spending a lot of time in the house where they now lived. Her time helping Joe and May Lentz, when May was so sick, was so vivid in her memory even though it was a long time ago.

When Martha had spare time she would crochet blankets or other things. They were handy to give for gifts. She said that when she grew old she would like to do more of that.

Amos and his oldest son now ran the carpentry crew. Lloyd was still helping them full time. The other boys helped too at times. With five boys and three daughters it took something to do to keep them all busy.

Sam was no longer going out to the job but spent his time working in the cabinet shop. Oscar worked there full time and hoped to someday take over the shop. Oscar's had three sons and two daughters.

Sam asked Amos if they would consider going to Indiana to their Love Feast. Amos said he would talk it over with Ellen. To go out of state to a Love Feast was something he didn't know if he wanted to do yet. When he talked to Ellen she said, "That would be enjoyable to see the family over there again."

Amos said, "Yes, but, It makes me sick in my stomach to think about having to speak."

Ellen said, "Your mother told me that is the way your father was the first time he went away."

Amos talked to Peter and he told him, "You need to go, the Lord be with you."

They had an enjoyable trip together. Since Sam and Amos were not working together anymore they didn't have the talks they used to. This trip gave them the opportunity to catch up on their visiting. Amos told his dad how he fretted about going out of state to a Love Feast.

Sam said, "I still have knots in my stomach at times. It's not the work, as much as it is the seriousness of handling the Holy Word of God. Therefore we must put our trust in Him and not think of ourselves."

Rob and Alice had eight boys and four girls. They lived on the farm which George Smith had owned when Sam worked for him one winter years ago. Their children's ages ran from two to seventeen with two sets of twins. Rob was a minister, and his brother Chuck a deacon. Together they farmed grain and livestock. Fred had purchased more land in hopes of keeping their children on the farm.

When they got to Rob and Alice's the children came running out, so glad to see them. Even though their grandparents and cousins had been there from time to time, and they had been to West Virginia several times over the years, the reunion was always a happy one.

They had a very nice meeting and were so built up in the faith. Sam and Amos were both happy they came as there was no doubt the Spirit was there.

They spent a couple days at Rob's. The children wanted Sam to tell them about his days in that house when he was young. He had told them about it several times, but they still wanted to hear it again. The younger children had never heard it from him, only what their siblings told them. Amos always put emphasis on the children doing what their parents told them. That saves a lot of sorrow.

Too soon it was time to give goodbyes. They had a nice trip home. They stopped twice to let the children run off their cramps. One of the stops was at a store in a small town close to the same trail that ran behind their house. There were a couple of hikers there getting supplies for the trail. Sam talked to them and told them about the place behind their house. He invited them to come on down to the house when they got there.

James was now a full time farmer. A few years ago he started doing gardening and selling it at the road, just a little at a time. The demand for direct off the farm produce was just becoming popular. The sales increased each year to the extent that he was able to quit carpentry and spent full time on the farm. They raised strawberries, and a lot of other vegetables, all of which were sold to the public at the stand.

Having seven children, James' needed work to keep them busy. Rachel, the oldest was now seventeen and was a wonderful help in the truck farming and seemed to enjoy it. When the busy season came she was the one that rounded up the help to harvest the produce. Wilma used to help, but now she spent most of her time in the house.

It had been five years since Charlie had left them. He kept getting weaker and although his mind was keen, his body wore out. One day, sitting in his recliner, he had slipped away. He left an empty spot in their home. They remembered the things he told them of trials in his life and the joys too. His bank took care of his affairs, and when all was settled up, he left five thousand to the church, three thousand to a charity and the rest to James. That finished paying off the farm.

Year after year time rolled by and now Sam was retired. He and Martha spent a lot of days in the summertime sitting on the porch swings. Their minds were good, however they repeated themselves sometimes. They always welcomed visitors. They especially enjoyed hearing singing from the hill behind their home. Occasionally they saw a hiker come to get water from the spring. Sam would go out and visit with them and invite them to rest on the front porch. If they needed anything, Martha would get it for them. Sam never met a stranger.

They were still active in the ministry and were always available to encourage those who were down. They seldom passed up an opportunity to go visit Rob and Alice and their grandchildren.

Sam had sold the cabinet shop to Oscar and he always had work for his family. Amanda came over as much as she could, but with grandchildren of her own she was busy a lot of the time.

James had plenty to do with the farm and the produce business. He was a deacon and had time to help those needing direction in their lives, both financially and emotionally. He and his family went through trying times of their own when Wilma came down with cancer. She suffered much while in the hospital for treatments. After six months of suffering, she passed away, leaving a grieving family. Rachel was eighteen and Steven had just turned seventeen. It was so hard for them to be brave and comfort the little ones when they wanted their mother. Martha came over often and the church members were so helpful.

Wilma's funeral was one of the saddest the Church had experienced since the three boys were shot many years prior. Enos came and helped Peter preach the service. It was hard for them to not break down, but they cast their eyes on the Lord who helps us in time of trouble. After the grave was filled, Peter said, "We can't stay here, The Lord has taken a loved one away. We will all go home and life will be somewhat normal. Please remember and pray for this family where normal will never be as it was before."

It was hard for James, and especially when they had their evening devotions. They tried hard to yield to the will of the Lord, knowing what the Lord does is well done.

Two years later James married Wilma's sister, Joan. This took some more adjusting but as Rachel had a wedding planned, and Steven was already married, the family was in need of a mother. This marriage was blessed with another son and two daughters. These additions gave the family ten children.

Sam had asked the church for more help in the ministry. They had strengthened the ministry when James was put in for a deacon, but now he and Raymond were getting old. They felt to keep brethren learning would keep the church strong. The Church chose Steven and his wife Julie for the ministry.

When they got home Martha said, "Do you think he can do it?"

Sam said, "Only with the help of the Lord."

Steven and Julie came over for some advice one evening. Sam and Martha gave them the same advice they gave to Amos and the others who had been given that responsibility. Steven asked about other changes happening in the world.

Sam said, "We are in a changing time, but God does not change. Be sure to live the commandments of Jesus, as they are written in the Bible. Only then will you preach them. Be sure to not lose your first love, as the church of Ephesus in the Revelations did. In the world that will likely happen. Be sure to yield to the Holy Spirit."

After they left, Martha said, "Maybe you should preach about the changes in the world and not in the church, before you get too old."

Sam said, "If the Spirit moves me to do so, I will."

That Sunday Sam asked for the second and third chapters of the Revelations to be read. James read them and Sam lined hymn number two-hundred, seventy-six.

Far down the ages now,
Much of her journey done,
The pilgrim church pursues her way,

Until her crown be won.

No wider is the gate,
 No broader is the way,
No smoother is the ancient path
 That leads to life and day.

No sweeter is the cup,
 Nor less our lot of ill,
'Twas tribulation ages since,
 'Tis tribulation still.

No slacker grows the fight,
 No feebler is the foe,
Nor less the need of armor tried
 Of shield, and spear, and bow.

Thus onward still we press,
 Through evil and through good-
Through pain and poverty, and want,
 Through peril and through blood.

Still faithful to our God,
 And to our Captain true,
We follow where he leads the way,
 The Kingdom in our view.

Sam looked around at the congregation and began to speak. "The Angel to the Church of Ephesus found fault with them, although they felt they were doing as they should. They had left their first love. How did this happen? Sometimes when man does well, Satan tells him how much better he is than others about him. Man has an inclination to think more of self than he ought. When this happens, he takes his eyes off the Lord, and focuses on himself. Satan loves that."

"As mortal beings, we of ourselves are weak. When Peter saw the Lord walking on the water he asked to let him come to Him. And he was able to do so as long as he kept his eyes on the Lord. Mortal man can't possibly walk on calm water, let alone the boisterous waves that were crashing around them that night. As soon as Peter took his eyes off of Jesus he started to sink."

"We are in changing times, and so to speak, the waves around us are getting boisterous. Of ourselves we will not be able to keep from sinking spiritually. Jesus says in Matthew twenty-four, verse twelve, *'And because iniquity shall abound, the love of many shall wax cold.'* How can this happen? In the prior verse He said, *'Many false prophets shall rise, and shall deceive many.'* This will bring on hatred. Man will get to where he will love only himself."

"Jesus said, 'The Gospel of the Kingdom shall be preached in the entire world.' Who is going to do that? Will it be someone who is selfish? Or will it be someone who never read the Bible? Or has a hateful attitude? No! Jesus told the people of the Church of Ephesus to repent and to do the first works. What are the first works? While Jesus doesn't say what they are in Revelations, He did say in Matthew to love the Lord thy God with all thy heart, soul, and mind. He also said to love thy neighbor as thyself. Back in Revelations, Jesus told the Church of Ephesus, *'He that overcometh will I give to eat of the tree of life, which is in the midst of the paradise of God.'*"

"How can we make sure we are a part of the people of God and are not being deceived by false prophets? It is by faith. Think of it as if the whole world was a boisterous sea, where there is no stability. As you look out across this sea, amongst the rough waves, you see Jesus with arms outstretched, saying 'Come unto me.' He is standing on the water. Slowly, with your eyes on Him, you start to walk towards your Savior. Your faith is strong and you doubt nothing as you walk right to Him. When you get to Him you are no longer on a boisterous sea. You are experiencing a great calm, as standing on a beautiful oasis. As you look out over the rough sea you see many folks floundering in the water. They are fighting each other, hating each other, cheating each other, killing each other. It goes on and on the atrocities they are committing."

"What can we do to warn others to flee from the things to come? Before Jesus went to the cross, He prayed a beautiful prayer recorded in John seventeen, and the last verse of that prayer He prayed, 'That the love wherewith thou hast loved me may be in them, and I in them.' Beloved, He has a desire to be in you. It is Christ in you, the hope of glory."

"We are attached to the vine. Jesus said, 'I am the vine, you are the branches.' As long as we stay attached to Him, keep our eyes on Him, put our full trust in Him, and love Him with all our heart, soul, strength and mind, we will be workers in His vineyard, pointing others to Him in the life we live. Then the boisterous, unstable sea waves of this world will not make us to doubt the salvation of the Lord."

"We have been a live church, a growing church, a loving church, and, yes, a suffering church. May we be a faithful church, then as the Church at Philadelphia, Jesus said, 'Because you have kept the word of my patience, I will keep you from the hour of temptation.' What we are calling the boisterous sea. Jesus continues in that verse 'which shall come upon all the world, to try them that dwell upon the earth.' Beloved we have hope of the promise, He will make us a pillar in the temple of His God, and we will go no more out. May we continue to live, so our lives may warn others on the boisterous sea, leading others to Jesus, that they perish not."

When Sam sat down it was so quiet you could hear a pin drop.

When Raymond closed he said, "If we all have as much love for the Lord as this brother has for you and the Lord, we will continue to strive harder to keep the faith. We have a wonderful flock here and it is still growing, but Satan will try in every way to destroy us. He destroyed the old meeting house, but the Lord has built three and may build more. He tried to discourage us by killing those who were fasting and praying for the guidance of the Holy Spirit. In return the Lord has increased our fellowship to three districts. Let us always continue to trust and obey."

Sam and Martha were now in their eighties. Steven and Julie moved in with them. Martha remembered the day they got married. They moved into this same house with Joe and May. She told Sam, "We are where Joe and May were when we got married. Now I know how May felt when someone else was in her kitchen."

Sam said, "It worked then, it will work now."

Sam and Martha now had over fifty offspring; no longer could they all be together in their home. In the summer time they used the shelter house in the park for their family gatherings, and in the winter they rented the conservation building. As much as they loved each of their loved ones, after they were all together for awhile, they needed to get some rest. They needed to go to where they could be alone for a spell.

Martha said, "Remember how we enjoyed the grandchildren when they were all together, but now it just gets on my nerves."

Sam said, "God knew what he was doing when he gave children to young people. Being in the sunset years of our lives, we need to be thankful to have our right minds."

One evening, as they were reminiscing over the past, Sam wanted to go for a drive over to the east meeting house. As they slowly drove down the winding drive, their minds were reflecting back over the years gone by. The joys and sorrows they had in those times. They parked, and as they walked by the meeting house, he said "Remember the day James and the twins were baptized here?"

Martha said, "All together there were nine baptized that day."

Sam said, "And they all have kept the faith so far. I think they will continue until God calls them home."

The fall leaves crunched under their feet as they walked through the grove of trees to the stream. It had been a long time since rocks had been placed in the stream creating the small pond to baptize. Now bubbling water ran down over the moss covered stones that made the pond where so many had made their commitment to the Lord. As they gazed into the reflection of the water Sam said, "Some of those who helped build this are now gone."

They walked through the cemetery looking at the stones and were amazed at how many stones were there. They talked about how there had been none there the day they built the meeting house. "That seems like such a short time ago," Martha said. "Think how many children don't know but this house has always been here."

They came to the bridge the members had built across the creek. Sam and Martha walked to the middle of the bridge and looked upstream for a while. Turning around they watched the water trickling over the rocks as it moved further downstream. After a few moments Sam said, "As the stream just keeps on flowing, so life does the same. To look upstream and to think where we came from, then to look down stream and to think where we are going. It makes me think of the hymn, *As flows the rapid river.*"

On the way back home they stopped by their meeting house. They walked from the parking lot up towards the church. "Remember the day we got married here?" Sam asked.

Martha smiled at Sam as she took his hand, "That is a day that is forever etched in my heart."

They walked on around the meeting house to the cemetery. They thought of how time passes so fast as they looked at the stones of their loved ones. They lived faithful lives, and are now waiting for the resurrection morning. They stood a while at the graves of the three boys who had been killed there years ago. Walking on down the row they came to their dear friends Jacob and Merial, Joe and May, Daniel and Amanda, and some others. They shed a few tears, as they thought of bygone days.

Martha said, "We had better go home as the sun is about to set." As they walked away, they started to hum *Beyond the Sunset*.

Back at home, they sat on the porch as the last of the twilight faded away. They were thinking of things as they currently were and how they used to be. Sam was the first to break the silence, "It is alright to think back behind us and to remember the influence we received from those loved ones, but it is important we also leave the same foot prints they left. They were only going one way, and that was to a home where we will never grow old." He had just finished speaking when some young folks, up at the camp ground started singing, *The land where we'll never grow old*.

Martha whispered, "Is that a coincidence, or is the Lord involved?"

Sam said, "The Spirit of our God is in them to remember us old people, and do what they know we so much enjoy."

The singing continued with four more songs they so much enjoyed. It greatly lifted their minds higher, when they heard the final song was *Rock of Ages*. They heard the young folks coming down the hill to the house and smiled a welcome as they gathered on the front porch. Then a couple of boys walked up with a freezer of ice-cream. The girls went into the house and brought dishes for Sam and Martha and served them. The rest had theirs in paper bowls they brought, using plastic spoons.

One of the older boys said, "Sam, would you tell us the story your father told you about the little red wagon stuck in the mud? There are young folks here now which have never heard you tell it."

Sam cleared his throat and brushed back a tear. He was thinking of his father, so long ago telling him and John that story, how he had said, "Pass it on boys." So as the young folks gathered around the porch swing on that brisk fall evening, Sam told the story. They were impressed and thanked him.

They bid them good night and Sam said, "Thank you for coming and singing, also for the ice-cream. May the Lord bless and keep you." As they were walking away, they started singing *God be with you until we meet again.*

Martha asked Sam after they left, "How many sheep do you want in your fold?"

He knew she was talking about the ewe lamb John had given him when he returned home. What his brother had told him came back as a reminder of the grace of God: *"Sam I forgive you for all you did and am giving you this lamb from the best of my flock, that someday you might have a flock of your own that will hear your voice."* Sam could not talk for a little as tears were streaming down his cheeks. Then, as he softly held Martha's hand, he said, "The Lord is our Shepherd. He is the true Shepherd, the good Shepherd. We are only his helpers, but I don't want any to go astray. When I think about the sheep I took care of when I was young, and how I loved them, little did I know what lay ahead. I love this flock even more than I did those."

After those thoughts settled, Sam continued, "I dread to think what might have happened had John not forgiven me. Where would I be now?"

Martha said, "You could have been in the gall of bitterness and the bond of iniquity."

Sam said, "I'm so thankful for godly parents who taught us to walk in the path of our Lord and Savior Jesus Christ."

The young folks were good about visiting the older folks in the district. Sometimes they would bring supper and other times just stop in, sing a few songs and visit with them. One day Amos commented to his mother, "You and dad started your married life taking care of Joe and May in their latter days, when others couldn't believe a newly married couple would do that. Since then several have followed that example of caring for older folks in their home."

Martha asked, "Did you feel underprivileged having Joe live with us?"

Amos responded, "In no way, but it was a blessing to have him around. I only wish I could have known May."

One time when the family was together, the grandchildren wanted to know about the first time Grandpa and Grandma saw each other. Grandpa said, "I was hiking on the trail up by the camp on my way home to my parent's home in Virginia. I stopped for a rest and to read my Bible. It was up where the camp is today. After some time of reading and meditating on what I had read, I started singing. It was a way of showing my appreciation for what the Lord had done for me. I had just finished singing *Rock of Ages* when Joe came up the hill and asked me to help them. They were both sick and badly needed help."

He told them the story of splitting wood and fixing supper for them and feeding soup to May. He explained how he had sat up with May all night so Joe could get some rest, how he had gone to the neighbors to tell them about Joe and May being sick and needing help. "I was about to leave when Joe convinced me to stay one more day. That evening the young people came and sang for them," Sam hesitated a little, and then said, "Martha

Jones was among those young people, but I didn't give her much thought at the time."

Martha said, "I was the girl that opened the door when a boy came and told my mother about Joe's needing help and I went down with her to their place. That night mother felt some should go and sing to Joe and May. So I got some of the young people together and we did that. I did notice that boy in his ragged overhauls and torn shirt sitting there. I also noticed he helped sing some of the songs and he had a deep voice and sang with enthusiasm most time. Sometimes he didn't sing, but wiped his eyes as if he were crying. May called him their angel. He looked more like a tramp to me, but he did help Joe and May over a rough night."

The Grandchildren said, "That's an interesting story, but how did you meet?"

Sam and Martha looked at each other smiling and Sam said, "That is another story, maybe you could ask your parents to tell you that one."

Martha asked, "Would you sing *Precious Memories*?"

So as they sang, Sam and Martha sang along, with tears in their eyes.

> *Precious father, loving mother*
> *Fly across the lonely years*
> *And old home scenes of my childhood*
> *In fond memory appears*

Sam was very feeble, but he wanted to go up to the campground one more time. The grandsons fixed a cart he could ride in and pulled him up the hill. He was happy to see it had been maintained and upgraded by the younger generation. He told them, "If you had not maintained this place it would have gone back to nature. It is the same with your spiritual life. From what I see, you are doing that, and the Lord is happy with you. Keep it up and pass it on."

Sam and Martha were very low. The children were all there. The Elders came and anointed both of them. They were in the same room Joe and May were in when they were anointed, the room Sam had built for them decades ago. A crowd, as many as could get there, was gathering up in the campground. Some of the older folks gathered on the porch. It was a very touching time as the flock he had overseen for so many years started singing, *Nearer my God to Thee*, and other songs they liked so well. Then someone noticed the carving on the log and pointing to it started singing *Rock of Ages*. As they were singing, *When I soar to worlds unknown*, Sam suddenly pointed upward and said "The angels!" and took his last breath.

When Martha saw that the man who had been by her side for most of her life was gone, she lost her desire to live any longer. She sobbed for a long time, and what little strength she still had ebbed from her worn body. Her children and others sat up with her that night. At about midnight Martha went into a coma and before morning she too passed into waiting hands of angels.

A few days later, the meeting house overflowed as the two caskets were rolled to the front of the church. Peter, although getting old, preached an emotional message of how "The sheep heard his voice."

After the funeral was all over and the family was at Steven and Julie's house, Amos and James, along with some of their boys, walked outside. Amos happened to see the old model A sitting among the weeds, the tires were flat, and one door was hanging down.

Amos asked James, "Do you remember the time Josh came down the road with this Model A and gave it to the folks?"

James said, "I sure do, that was a long time ago." The memories made them cry.

Amos said, "Dad would say, 'That is what life will do to you, if you let the weeds of the world grow and not maintain your Christian walk.'"

James said, "I'll say Amen to that."

The End

CPSIA information can be obtained
at www.ICGtesting.com
Printed in the USA
FFHW020158261118
49485568-53868FF